wake
the
stone
man

wake
the
stone
man

a novel by
Carol McDougall

Roseway Publishing
an imprint of Fernwood Publishing
Halifax & Winnipeg

Editing: Chris Benjamin & Brenda Conroy
Cover image: Sleeping Giant, Fort William, Ontario Postcard
Design: John van der Woude
Printed and bound in Canada

Published by Roseway Publishing
an imprint of Fernwood Publishing
32 Oceanvista Lane, Black Point, Nova Scotia, BOJ 1BO
and 748 Broadway Avenue, Winnipeg, Manitoba, R3G 0X3
www.fernwoodpublishing.ca/roseway

Fernwood Publishing Company Limited gratefully acknowledges the
financial support of the Government of Canada through the Canada Book
Fund, the Canada Council for the Arts, the Nova Scotia Department of
Tourism and Culture and the Province of Manitoba, through the Book
Publishing Tax Credit, for our publishing program.

Library and Archives Canada Cataloguing in Publication

McDougall, Carol, author
Wake the stone man / Carol McDougall.

Issued in print and electronic formats.
ISBN 978-1-55266-721-7 (pbk.).--ISBN 978-1-55266-764-4 (epub)

I. Title.

PS8625.D776W36 2015   C813'.6   C2015-900603-1
                             C2015-900604-X

For my family of friends.
Love is all there is.

book one

chapter one

The first time I saw her she was climbing over the top of the chain-link fence of the residential school. The tops of her fingers curled over the metal fence were dark, but the palms facing me were pink. Pink as mine. I wanted to look down at mine to check, but she was staring at me. I waited for her to speak. She didn't.

I could have kept walking, should have kept walking down the path to the building where I took my ballet lessons. Didn't have to stop just because she was staring at me. But I stopped and watched her.

"Nakina!" A flash of black behind her as a nun moved towards the fence. Black and white, and the glint of silver from the buckle of a belt. "Get off that fence."

Thwack of metal as the buckle hit the fence.

I ran. I ran down the path, away from the residential school, ballet shoes bouncing off my back. I was on the other side of that fence and I didn't have a strap coming down on my back but I ran like hell. She didn't move.

After that day I looked for her. I wanted to ask her some-thing. I wanted to ask her where she was going that day she tried to escape over the fence. Every time I went to my dance class I stopped outside the fence to see if I could find her.

Some people called St. Mary's the residential school. My mom called it the orphanage. I asked her what it meant and she said it was a place for orphans, and I said what's an orphan and she said someone whose parents are dead, and I said are all those Indian kids' parents' dead and she said no. I didn't get it.

The place was huge. Bigger than the church and bigger than City Hall. A red brick building four storeys high, with rows and rows of narrow windows and a porch on the sec-ond floor. Indian kids lived there. Mostly Indian, looked like hundreds of them. And the nuns who ran the place were always yelling and making them line up. Nuns in long black robes screaming their heads off. Scary.

I stopped every time I walked by. I saw kids playing mar-bles under a statue of Jesus nailed to the cross. In winter I saw kids playing hockey on the rink they'd made in the field behind the school. In spring I saw kids working in the gardens and lining up to go in for mass when the bells in the chapel rang. But I didn't see her.

⸻

The summer I was eleven everything changed. One minute I'm sitting on the dock, swinging my skinny little legs over the side, the next I'm standing up looking at the Sleeping Giant, thinking what the hell—what the hell am I doing here?

I looked back at the rust bleeding down the side of Sask.

Pool 7. I looked at the fat rats waddling along the tracks beside the grain elevators. I looked at the thick green slime pouring out of the mill into the Kamanistiquia River. And it felt like I was looking at one of those ink blob pictures—first you see two faces nose-to-nose and suddenly you're looking at a goddamned vase. Zap. I don't know how the faces changed into a vase; all I know is after I saw the vase I couldn't see the faces any more. One minute Fort McKay looked like home. Then zap, it looked like a hick town in the middle of the bush and I wanted out.

It was 1964 and stuff was happening out there, out past the Sleeping Giant across Lake Superior in the good ole U. S. of A. We watched it every night on the news. Martin Luther King had a dream; Kennedy got shot and bled all over his wife in the pillbox hat. Nice hat.

I remember my teacher running into the classroom screaming, "Our president's been shot." I don't know what was weirder, that she thought he was *our* president or that I believed her. She told us all to go home, and I remember kids running down the halls screaming like there'd been a nuclear attack. Which, by the way, was another thing we were all freaking out about.

Things were happening. Every night on TV I watched guys getting blown up in Vietnam. I was learning new words like Viet Cong, Saigon, napalm bomb. One night we were eating barbequed hot dogs off TV tables and I watched this Buddhist monk tip a tin of gasoline over his head. He was sitting cross-legged on the road and whoosh, he went up in flames. Barbequed hot dog with barbequed monk. Stuff was happening out there. But I wasn't out there. I was stuck in the middle of nowhere.

That day, when I was eleven, I waited on the wharf till my dad brought the boat around and we headed out through the breakwater past the lighthouse. The Merc engine kicked up a cold spray on my face. I looked back at the harbour as we pulled out and I could see the whole of Fort McKay broken down—North Fort and South Fort and the mountains. From out there you could see lines you couldn't see in town. North Fort McKay. Money. Where my aunt and uncle lived and drank martinis with people like them who thought their shit didn't stink. My Uncle Pete was such an asshole. Seriously, he was just a foreman at the mill but he thought he was the friggin Duke of Duluth. Everyone in North Fort McKay looked down on people who lived in South Fort McKay, who looked down on people who lived in West Fort McKay, where I lived. I lived in a cardboard-box house that looked just like all the other cardboard boxes on the street. They called them wartime houses, which made no sense to me because there wasn't a war on, except for the Vietnam War, and I couldn't see how my house had anything to do with that.

West Fort was bad, but it wasn't the bottom of the barrel. The bottom of the barrel was the South Fort Reserve, on the other side of the swing bridge. Everyone crapped on them, but they had no one downwind of them to crap on.

I could see all that as the boat pulled away from the city out onto Lake Superior. My dad built the boat. He used to race hydroplanes but he couldn't any more because he was a father and had responsibilities. Me. My mother made him give up racing so he built a nice little boat we could all toodle around in, except when it was done it looked a lot like a hydroplane racer. Ha. Dad put a 75 Merc on the back of that thing and man could she go. Dad's racing buddy Aho Sippo used to say, "That Merc really put the poop in 'er."

It was sunny when we headed out. Dad didn't bother to tell Mom we were going out because he thought we'd just do a spin past the Giant. But when we got near the Welcome Islands the sky went dark and the lake churned up fast. Superior did that. It would be calm as glass one minute then spitting up whitecaps the next. The sky went black, then lit up with forks of lightning. We were too far out when the storm hit to get into one of the bays along the shore. Dad shouted to me to get under the bow. The wind was blowing his curly red hair back off his face and his long body was curled over the engine. Dad kept a bunch of blankets and extra life jackets under the bow and I crawled into them like a nest. Couldn't see anything, but I knew the waves were breaking high because the bow would dip down a few feet, smash and fly up again. The Merc was full throttle and the rain was pounding on the deck. I wasn't scared. You'd think I'd be scared out there in a storm like that, but I wasn't. Being stuffed under the deck was like being tucked safe inside a kangaroo pouch. I never worried because I knew no matter how rough it got my dad could ride it out.

The only thing the storm did was rock me to sleep, and when I woke up we were coming through the breakwater. It was dark. I could see the blinking of the lighthouse and the lights of a police boat following us in. Police were waiting on the dock. Mom called them when we didn't come home. There were a lot of guys in uniforms and lights and questions, and I just wanted to go home and go to back to sleep.

At home Mom grabbed me and sobbed her face out. Then she started in on my dad. See, Mom was usually real quiet. Dad called her his rock because she was always so calm, so it was a big flippin deal when she lost it. She was standing in the kitchen beside a stack of dishes and she just picked one up and let fly. Dad ducked and it smashed against the wall behind him. She kept throwing plates. Dad kept ducking. I wondered why he didn't get the heck out of the way. I guess he was like me—deer caught in the headlights. I wanted to know what it felt like to haul off and swing a plate across the room. Must have felt good. And bad. I didn't ask. I went to bed.

That night I dreamt about waking the Stone Man—Nanna Bijou, the Sleeping Giant. I dreamt about him a lot. The Giant is a mountain of stone that sticks out into the harbour. Looks just like a man lying down with his arms crossed over his chest. When you grow up in Fort McKay the Giant gets under your skin and inside your head.

That night I dreamt I was standing on the wharf shouting my guts out across the harbour and there was this god-awful crash of rocks and the Stone Man sat up and looked at me, all surprised. And I threw my hands up and said, "What the hell!" I waited for him to say something profound but he just smiled and gave me a "Hey, how's it going, eh?" sort of nod, then lay back down across the harbour and folded his arms across his chest.

———

I was a weird kid. Didn't talk much, so people forgot I was there. When I was little people thought I was like Donny MacKellvey. He chased lawnmowers. As soon as someone on the street would pull the starter on a lawnmower Donny would be right there, watching like it was the Stanley Cup playoffs. People called Donny mongoloid, but I knew his family wasn't from Mongolia. People used to think I was like Donny so they didn't pay any attention when I was around. That was OK by me. I heard more that way.

I heard how Mr. Rutka crossed the dockworker's picket line on purpose, and they said he was a scab and was going to pay for it. I heard how Mr. Abromovitch invited all the neighbours to his house on Christmas Eve so they could watch him kill his wife. He drove his car to our house to ask my dad to come over for a drink, which was nuts because he lived across the street. When my dad said he couldn't go, Mr. Abromovitch left his car in our driveway because he was so drunk he didn't remember driving over. His car was still at our house when the police took him away for shooting his wife. The bullet just grazed her ear so she wasn't dead. Just stunned. But I always thought she was stunned. One of his sons came a few days later and got the car.

I used to go to church every Sunday morning with Mom and Dad. I'd go to Sunday school downstairs for the first half hour, then we'd go upstairs with our families for the church service. I liked church. I liked the smell of wood and wax. I liked the organ music and I could belt out the hymns with the best of them. I was sitting in church when I heard some men in the pew in front of me bragging about "taking care" of some guy on the reserve, and then they all laughed a lot. I didn't know what they were talking about but I knew I didn't like it—or them.

Someone stole my winter boots from the front vestibule when I was downstairs one Sunday. After that I stopped going to church. It was partly because of the boots, I mean, come on—how the heck can you say you're a Christian and steal someone's boots? But it was also the stuff I heard. I'd sit in the pew listening to all this stuff about what *really* went on, which didn't sound anything like what the minister said was *supposed* to be going on, so I figured there was no god. Well at least not in Fort McKay. So I stopped going.

Instead I hung out in Paula Slobokin's kitchen on Sundays while her baba made perogies and cabbage rolls and little pastry things she would make me eat because she said I was too skinny. She'd slap my hips and say "Wide hips. Lots of babies." I hated that but I liked the perogies. Baba told us stories about the Ukraine, the old country, which was weird because my nana used to tell me stories about the old country, which she called Scotland, and Anna's mummo called her old country Finland. When I was a kid I used to think the old country was on the other side of Mount McKay, and people wore kilts and had Ukrainian wedding ribbons in their hair and rode around on reindeer. Eventually I figured out there was no old country on the other side of the mountain—just trees, trees and more friggin trees.

On summer nights I'd sit out on the front steps with my mom and dad looking across at the neighbours who were sitting on their front steps looking across at us. Real exciting. Donny used to come over and sit with us. He never said much but I liked hanging out with Donny. You always knew where you stood with him. I'd sit there breathing in the rotten-egg sulfur stink of the mill, playing snakes and ladders with Donny and wondering what people in places like Toronto and Winnipeg and New York were doing.

I'd sit on the steps thinking about how I was going to

get out of Fort McKay and wondering if everyone else sitting on their steps was thinking the same thing. Hard to tell. Seemed to me they were all pretty happy where they were. Reggie Dalmino's dad worked at the mill and Reggie wanted to work at the mill. His twin brother Ace wanted to, you got it, work at the mill. The girls I hung out with sang skipping songs about who-am-I-going-to-marry and how-many-kids-am-I-going-to-have. Except in Fort McKay it was usually the other way around: how many kids am I going to have and is the bastard going to marry me? Aim high. But that was the thing. For most of my friends that *was* aiming high. There's this saying here…good enough. When someone says "Hey, howya doing?" you say "goodnuff." "See you at bingo next week." "Goodnuff." Life may not be great, but hey, it's goodnuff.

But that summer I decided goodnuff wasn't good enough for me. I wanted more. I wanted out. I kept thinking about the girl I'd seen trying to escape over the fence of the residential school. I figured she wanted out too.

chapter two

It was two years before I saw her again. I'd been sick the first week of high school so I had to go to the office to register. I was waiting outside the principal's office feeling so nervous I thought I would puke, when she walked over, sat down beside me and said, "Hi," just like that. Hadn't seen her since the day she was trying to escape from the residential school, and she looked right at me and said "Hi" like we were best friends or something.

"Nakina Wabasoon?" The principal stuck his head out of his office. "Come on in." After a couple of minutes the principal came back out and nodded to me.

"Molly Bell? Come in."

I went in and sat down in a chair beside Nakina. The principal was short and fat and had a wonky eye so you never knew if he was looking at you.

He went through a lot of stuff about teachers and lockers and wings and periods and I kept nodding my head like an idiot. I was nodding and smiling and wondering which one of his eyes was the real one and which was the glass one, and I didn't know what the hell he was saying.

Before we left his office he said to Nakina, "I see here on your file that you have epilepsy."

"Yes." She looked at me and I could tell she didn't like him saying that in front of me.

"I'm going to set up an appointment for you to meet with the school nurse. You can let her know about your medication and give her your doctor's name."

"OK."

"Oh, and Molly."

"Yes?" I said.

"I want you to go with Nakina to the nurse. Since you're in the same homeroom you'll know what to do if she has a seizure."

"OK."

Outside the office door I turned to Nakina and said, "So, what's epilepsy?"

"You'll find out," she said.

I was just about to tell Nakina that I didn't have a clue where we were supposed to go and she said, "Follow me."

So I followed her down the corridor. I followed her to our lockers. I followed her to our homeroom. And after that day, I just kept following Nakina.

We were both in Mrs. Kouie's English class. English for girls in secretarial arts and cosmetology. Cosmetology—I remember getting real excited about that till I found out it had nothing to do with the theory of the universe.

I liked English. Liked books. Never told anyone but my favourite place was the Brodie Street Library. I used to sit at the table under a stained glass window with two big heads—Charles Dickens and William Shakespeare. I liked sitting with Charlie and Billy.

Mrs. Kouie loved words, metaphors and allegories. She loved poets. But most of all Mrs. Kouie loved Leonard. Mrs. Kouie let us borrow her poetry books, and on our lunch break Nakina and I would find an empty classroom and read Leonard. Then we wrote the poems in chalk on the board to see the shape of the words of Leonard Cohen.

Nakina discovered *The Spice-Box of the Earth* and began to read aloud "For you I will be a Dachau Jew and lie down in lime with twisted limbs..."

"That's me," she said.

"He's writing about Jews. Are you a Jew?"

"He's writing about the holocaust."

"Are you a holocaust Jew?" I asked.

"Yes."

"Get out."

"I am."

"Get out."

"He means Jews metaphorically."

"You're a metaphorical Jew?"

"Don't be an ass, Molly."

"Seriously, I don't get how you are metaphorically a Jew."

"I'm Indian. Anishinaabe."

"So."

"So we're like the Jews. The Jews of Canada."

"You're a Canadian, Indian Jew. OK, so what about the holocaust?"

"Do you even know what a holocaust is?"

"Sure, what happened to the Jews in the war."

"No. The word. Do you know what the word means?"

I shrugged.

"Genocide. The slaughter of a race. What they did to me."

"Come on. Who slaughtered you?"

"The residential school."

"I don't get it. How?"

"Red kids in—white kids out. Genocide."

I got quiet after that. Didn't know what to say. Just got up and went back to class. Couldn't concentrate on anything all afternoon.

Red kids in—white kids out. I kept thinking about the first time I saw Nakina, climbing the chain link fence trying to escape with the belt coming down on her back. Leather belt coming down to whack the Indian right out of her.

———◈———

Nakina started coming home with me. Don't remember if I invited her or if she just came home with me one day and kept on coming. She was living with a foster family in Rosslyn Village then. The Dekkers. Dutch family who ran a milk farm. When she came home with me for dinner she usually stayed overnight, which was fine by me.

Nakina loved cards and cribbage, which I hated, so she was a hit with Mom and Dad. They would sit around the table all night drinking pots of tea and yapping away, playing cards. Dad would sit there with a cigarette on the go and Mom would have her hair up in curlers and Nakina would have a bowl of popcorn in front of her.

Me, I'd curl up on the couch with a book. Books were how I got my kicks. Mrs. Comusi across the street drank. She'd sit out on the steps in the summer with her magazines and gin, and by the time the street lights came on she'd be dancing like a rag doll across the lawn shouting at the neighbour men to come and join her. She was happy as a pig in shit and everyone knew it was the gin. But hey, what the hell. Gin did it for her, books did it for me. By high school I had a four-book-a-week habit.

It was nice having one more warm body in the family. With just me around it got boring. I bored myself. Too quiet, too shy, too scared of my own shadow. Nakina was a kick in the ass.

Our family sure needed it. When I was ten my mom got pregnant. I was excited about having another kid in the family, but when she came back from the hospital there was no baby. Nobody told me what happened. No one ever spoke about it and somehow I knew I couldn't ask. She got quiet after that and it got harder to talk to her. People kept telling my mom how sorry they were, but they forgot she wasn't the only one in the family who lost that baby.

When Nakina started coming home with me things got better. She was funny and said stuff I could never get away with. Like one time at dinner my dad was asking if she helped out on the Dekkers' farm.

"Yeah. Last week they let me help band the calves."

"What's that?" I asked. Big mistake.

"You lay the calf down on the ground, tie its legs together, then grab the balls in one hand and this metal thing with an elastic band in the other. Then you put the elastic band over their balls and zap them right off."

I thought that was hilarious. I mean, seriously, she said "zap their balls off" at the dinner table, which cracked me up so I kept laughing, and guess who got into trouble.

Nakina would sit at the table when mom was cooking, peeling potatoes for her and asking questions. Like she was doing research on families. On *my* family. I listened. It looked like I was reading but I was listening. Listening to my mom talk about how she could see the grain boats out the window of her bedroom at the top of Grandma's house in North Fort when she was a little girl; how they made Spitfires at the Auto Works during the war; how she met my dad at a dance at the officers club. She told Nakina about how she and my dad moved to a cabin north of Nipigon after they were married and how my dad and his friend caught sturgeon and sold caviar to a store in New York. People paid a lot of money to eat fish eggs. Gross! My mom talked about her friend Martha, who was Ojibwe and had a trapline with her family near our cabin. I don't know why my mom never told me any of this stuff. Guess I never asked.

I looked at Mom and Nakina standing together at the sink and I thought they looked more like mother and daughter than my mom and me. Nakina was the same height as Mom, and they both had long black hair pulled into a loose ponytail. And they were both—I don't know—round, and curvy. I looked down at my stick legs and flat chest. Lucky me, I inherited my father's chest.

That night when Nakina was playing cards with Dad I helped Mom wash the dishes.

"How old was I when we moved back here from the cabin?" I asked.

"Oh, you were going on five. You started school that fall."

"Is that why you moved back?" I asked.

"Partly. Dad's business wasn't going too well, and I missed the city."

"I remember my bed at the cabin—it was like a princess bed with a frame covered in white lace."

"Not lace, mosquito netting."

"It felt like a princess bed to me. "

"When you were a baby my friend Martha showed me how to string a hammock between the beams of the cabin. It kept you up high where it was warmer, and away from the mice."

"Did you like living there?" I asked.

"Sometimes. It was hard, but we were happy." Her voice trailed off and she seemed to be getting sad so I didn't ask anything else.

That night when Nakina and I were in bed reading I turned to her and asked, "What are you going to do?"

"What?" She looked over the top of her book at me.

"What are you going to do?" I asked again.

"When?"

"When you get out of here?"

"Out of where?" she said.

"Here."

"This room?" she said.

"No, idiot."

"Out of where?"

"Fort McKay."

"Trying to get rid of me?"

"Come on. Seriously." I put down my book on the French Impressionists and looked across at Nakina.

"Dunno. Haven't thought about it," she said.

"Want to know where I'm going?"

"No."

"Paris. I'm going to go to the Moulin Rouge, where

Toulouse-Lautrec hung out, and to the Louvre to see the Cezannes."

"Oh yeah?"

"Yeah. And I'm going to live in an attic in the Latin Quarter with my French lover and paint all day."

"Very funny."

"I'm serious," I said.

"What's the point of making plans. You'll never get out of Fort McKay."

"I will."

"You won't."

"I will."

"You never will."

"Shut up." I closed my book.

"Hey Nakina."

"Yeah."

"You know that first day I saw you."

"In the principal's office?"

"No, that day you were trying to get over the fence at the residential school."

"Yeah."

"Where were you going?"

"Home," she said.

"Where's home?"

"Dunno."

"Oh." I put my book down and turned off the light. "Hey Nakina."

"What."

"Well, if you didn't know where home was…"

"Yeah?"

"Well, how were you going to find it?"

"God, Molly."

"No, really. What were you going to do when you hit the ground on the other side of the fence?"

Nakina rolled over and sat up on one arm. "Find the tracks."

"The tracks?" I asked.

"Yeah. Tracks."

"What tracks?"

"Train tracks, genius."

"Fuck off!" I closed my eyes and tried to go to sleep but I couldn't stop thinking. "Hey Nakina?"

"What?"

"Why were you going to find the train tracks?"

"Because that's all I remember. A train."

"What train?"

"I remember a train that came through the bush stealing kids. Taking us away."

"Away where?'

"Here, I guess."

"And that's why you were going to find the tracks?"

"Yeah."

"But I still don't get it. How would that help you get home?"

"Tracks run both ways."

"Oh. Hey Nakina?"

"What."

"Good thinking."

———◆———

I was sitting on the front steps with Nakina playing cat's cradle. She held her hands up in front of her and I looped a long circle of string in and out of her fingers to make a star shape. It was cold. Winter was in the air and the grass crunched when you walked on it.

Bernie Olfson, the cop who lived a few houses down from us, drove into his driveway and I could see antlers sticking out from the back of his truck. There's something about a guy driving up the street with a moose in the back of his truck that sets off a silent alarm. One minute there was no one on the street except Nakina and me, the next all the dads were at their doors. They didn't go over right away. First they stood on their steps, arms crossed, like they'd just stepped outside to get a breath of fresh air. Then they looked over at Mr. Olfson casually and gave him the Fort McKay how-ya-doing-eh nod. Then after a bit they strolled over to his place and said "Hey, so you got yer moose."

Before long my dad and six other guys were helping Mr. Olfson lift the moose out of the truck. They set it down on the middle of his lawn and then stood around, waiting.

After a while Nakina and I walked over and joined some other kids on the sidewalk. I'd seen my dad skin rabbits when we lived up north, but I was curious about how they'd skin something as big as a moose. It was lying on its side, head tilted back and its big grey tongue hanging out. It looked gross.

"So what do you say Bernie, he's about, what…a thousand pounds?" my dad asked.

"Bit more I'd say. Maybe fifteen hundred."

Mr. Olfson had two knives. One was about twelve inches long and the other not much bigger than a pocket knife. Looked pretty small to skin such a big thing.

The men stepped back and watched Mr. Olfson make

the first cut. First he took the long knife and sliced off the head. Blood gushed out all over his boots. A few guys lifted the severed head and tossed it towards where we were standing. Steam was rising from the head as the hot blood hit the cold air. Some boys turned to look at me and Nakina. I think they thought we were going to scream or puke or something, but we just kept watching.

Mr. Olfson took the smaller knife and cut just above the tail and slid the knife under the hide and started peeling back the skin. At that point a few of the men knelt down around the moose and helped fold the skin back as he cut. When they had exposed one side they rolled the moose over and skinned the other side. Then one of the guys picked up the skin in a heap and dropped it beside the head.

My dad went into Mr. Olfson's garage and came back with some rope and they rolled the moose onto its back. My dad wrapped the rope around one of the front feet just above the hoof and tied a knot. He tied the other end to the tree. One of the other guys tied up the other front leg to the back of the truck. The moose was lying headless on its back, front feet splayed between the tree and the back of the truck. With the skin pulled off you could see every red sinewy muscle.

Mr. Olfson cut down its throat and pulled up the trachea. Then he cut into the belly, careful not to go too deep, and a few of the guys rolled up their sleeves, stuck their arms into the belly and pulled out a long twisted tube of intestines. They laid the intestines beside the carcass and white steam rose from the hot belly.

Mr. Olfson went into his garage, and with bloody hands he carried out a small chainsaw. He pulled the starter chord and when the engine kicked in he made a cut through the ribs.

I guess Donny must have heard the chainsaw start up because he came out of his house and walked towards Mr. Olfson's. My dad was helping them pull the ribs apart. Mr. Olfson grabbed the throat and pulled down slowly, bringing all the internal organs out—lungs, heart and stomach.

Donny came up beside me, and when he saw all the blood he started rocking back and forth and moaning. I turned him around and put his head on my shoulder so he wouldn't see. Nakina said we should take him home, so we walked him back to his house and hung out with him for a while.

It was getting dark when we went home but Mr. Olfson's garage door was open and the light was on. You could see the headless moose carcass, back legs tied together, hanging from the ceiling of the garage.

chapter three

The Beatles were coming. *A Hard Day's Night* finally hit the boonies and Nakina and I went to Woolworths to buy make-up. Had to look good.

Nakina picked out pink lipstick. I wasn't into lipstick so I stood there wondering why Woolworths smelled like old men's socks. I saw the salesclerk watching us. It happened every time I went shopping with Nakina.

First there were the raised eyebrows that said she knew there was an Indian kid in the store. Then the eyebrows would lower and she'd look like she just sucked on a lemon. Then she'd cross her arms across her chest, and I would start counting to myself…one, two, three…and over she comes. This clerk came up to us and said, "Can I help you?" and I said, "No, just looking," and she said, "Well, you have to leave the store if you're not going to buy anything." Nakina held up a lipstick and said, "I'm buying this."

The woman followed us to the cashier and waited until

Nakina paid for the lipstick. They wanted her out but not before they got their money. You gotta love this town.

On the big day we walked into town. Nakina wore the new pink lipstick. It looked good on her.

There was one good thing about South Fort, they had not one, but two—count 'em—two movie theatres—the Odeon and the Capital. North Fort only had one—ha.

We sang all the way into town with arms linked, shouting at the top of our lungs: "When I saw her staan-ding there." We swung our heads as we sang so our hair would flip around. Nakina's hair was straight so it really flew but mine was like a frizzy pot scrubber so it just wiggled. We were still singing when we got to the theatre.

It was dark when we went in but I remember thinking something was weird. I expected to see a lot of kids from school but the theatre was almost empty. The maroon velvet curtain opened. And the first thing I saw were the credits: *Histoire…nuit et Brouillard*. What the hell. French? That was the first clue.

After the credits rolled there was this big green field. Nice. And nothing happened. I waited for four guys in black suits to pop up on the horizon and run across the field. Then the camera moved back, and farther back, and I was looking at the field from behind a barbed wire fence. Then music, flutes and violins, and a man's deep voice speaking in French and there were subtitles across the bottom: "The blood has dried, the tongues have fallen silent."

The camera panned back farther behind the fence and I saw rows of buildings with tall brick chimneys. The man was speaking again—names like Auschwitz and Bergen-Belsen. I didn't know what it meant, but I was pretty sure that Paul,

John, George and Ringo weren't going to come running across that green field.

The next shot was a crowd of people and some little guy in a uniform was shouting at them, and as his arm shot up into the air Nakina punched me in the shoulder. "What the hell, Molly!"

I looked at her with raised eyebrows because I really didn't know what to say, and she hissed, "The Capital you idiot, the Capital Theatre."

She punched me again "Get up. *Now!*"

Nakina stood and pushed past me, grabbing my sweater as she went, but I didn't move. At the end of the aisle she pushed past an old man and woman and they grumbled at her. I saw her shadow move up the aisle towards the door. I didn't move. Couldn't. It was too late.

I looked back up at the screen and saw long low buildings behind barbed wire. At the end was a big brick building. I tried to read the subtitles but they went by too fast. They were like weird poems.

I saw crowds of people standing at a train station. A row of children, alone. I wondered where their parents were. Maybe it was a school trip? But they looked scared and I knew it wasn't a school trip. Maybe they were being sent away because of the war? I had heard about kids from England being sent to Canada during the war. Maybe these kids were being sent away to keep them safe.

I watched them getting on the train, not into the passenger cars—they went into the big open baggage cars. More and more and more kids. Some guy in a uniform pulled the sliding door across. I saw a face in the crack just before it closed. The face of a girl about my age with a scarf on her head. Her eyes were big white circles. The guy in the uniform pulled the door again and the girl's face disappeared. He bolted the door closed. More trains, more people, more guys in uniforms with dogs. The camera pulled back to a shot from above showing the train moving across a field. Then night, and searchlights pointed at the train. The doors opened and bodies fell out. I thought they must have fainted because there were so many people crammed together on the train. Lines of people were loaded into big open-backed trucks. Trucks moved through the night and fog towards a building. A building that looked like the residential school.

Then men. I saw naked men. Stark naked. I'd never seen a naked man before. I'd seen girls at swimming class in the change room but never a naked man. I saw a long line of old naked men facing me and I thought oh god, oh god what kind of a movie did I walk into? I looked down the aisle to see if I could squeeze past the couple at the end. Their knees were sticking out so far I wouldn't be able to get past them. I looked to my left. A few men were sitting at the end of the aisle. In front another man and woman—they looked old—and beside them some men were sitting alone.

I looked up again. Shaved heads. Striped pajamas. Inside the long low buildings, rows and rows of bunk beds stacked with people like chickens in a chicken coup. A woman's big white scared eyes, like the eyes of the girl on the train. The music was creepy and sad.

The barbed wire fence again, and there was a man hanging on it, the tops of his fingers curled over the fence. Curled over like Nakina's fingers the day I saw her climbing the chain-link fence. His head was tilted back, a hole through his forehead, and because the movie was in black and white the blood that dripped down his cheek was black. The camera pulled back and I saw that he was hanging dead on the fence, hooked there by the collar of his coat.

Rows and rows of men and boys—naked again but this time their legs were thin and I could see their ribs, and I didn't think it was dirty that they were naked because their faces were so sad and their bodies so thin, and their penises were small and shrivelled. I wanted to wrap them in warm blankets.

I saw a country cottage. A man in a uniform with a swastika on his shoulder and a woman in a flower print dress were having tea in front of the fireplace. There was a dog beside them. The woman looked bored.

I saw the date 1942 on the screen, then more men in uniforms looking at a model of a building with a brick chimney. More trains, more trucks and women and children herded naked into the buildings with the chimneys—then bodies on the floor. I couldn't look at the subtitles anymore, I couldn't take my eyes off the children. Now women and children were standing in a field in front of a firing squad. There was a crack of fire as the guns went off and the women and children fell. A muffled cry, then weeping. Was it me? No, the older woman two rows down in front of me was crying. She had her head on the shoulder of the man beside her.

A body in a bed. He was dead but his eyes were wide open. That terror look again—the eyes all white. I wanted to close my eyes but I couldn't. Piles of eyeglasses and combs, and the camera panned back to show a large pile of human hair then farther back to show a wide field of human hair. Furnace doors opened and human bones were shovelled out. I remembered what Nakina had said—genocide—the slaughter of a race.

Piles of body parts, unattached legs still wearing socks, hands over legs over heads. A tin pail of men's heads, all with their eyes open. A head upside down with a big black hole where an eye should have been. Then a tractor. It moved slowly, slowly forward, scooping up bodies in its shovel. Forward slowly, arms, legs, ribs, heads rolled and writhed in a strange dance. A muffled scream and this time it was me.

There was colour now. Green. The wide green field. And below the words: "Who amongst us will keep watch for the *new* executioner? Who amongst us will keep watch?"

The lights came on in the theatre and I lowered my head and closed my eyes. I could hear the people shuffling out. I waited until it was silent, then I waited a few moments longer before moving out into the bright sun of the afternoon.

Standing at the corner of Main Street I could see both theatres. The marquee of the Odeon Theatre read *Night and Fog* and the marquee of the Capital Theatre read *A Hard Day's Night*.

I dreamt about the Stone Man that night. He was standing in the harbour holding the hand of a little girl. The girl I'd seen on the train before the door slid shut. The girl with the scarf over her head and big white scared eyes. I could see her lips open just a bit, like she was trying to say something to me, but before I could hear what she was saying the Stone Man let go of her hand, and she sank slowly into Lake Superior. I woke up screaming and when I finally got back to sleep I dreamt I saw the Stone Man again, holding a bucket towards me. I looked in the bucket and saw a bunch of heads, some of them with black holes where their eyes should have been. The faces smiled and started singing, "It's been a hard day's night."

I never told mom and dad about the movie. Don't know why. Just didn't, or couldn't. Just went on with the same old, same old. We ate dinner on TV tables watching new stuff burn on the five o'clock news: burning bras, burning draft cards and Quakers, who started burning themselves on the streets like the Buddhist monks. Toasted Quaker Oats.

I watched *A Charlie Brown Christmas* on TV. I liked his big sad head. After a while the nightmares went away.

chapter four

stepped off the curb and stood in the middle of First Avenue holding my brownie camera in front of my face. "Nakina!"

"What?"

"I said watch for cars."

"Why?"

"Because I'm trying to take a freakin photo and I don't want to get run over."

I was creating my masterpiece. It was 4 p.m. on March 25, 1968, and I was capturing Fort McKay for posterity. Well, maybe not posterity—I just wanted to freeze-frame what I was looking at right there the way it was. No smoke and mirrors, just the main street of the town in the raw. I shot in black and white and tried to keep everything simple. I took a photo of the clock in the Empire tower and the basket man pushing a baby carriage full of wicker baskets in front of the hardware store. I took a photo of Mary Christmas.

I never knew what her real name was, but everyone called her Mary Christmas because she wore these red and green ribbons in her hair. She was pretty festive with her make-up too. She painted bright red circles on her cheeks and when she put on her ruby red lipstick she drew outside the lines. She was old and wore a ratty fur coat that almost touched the ground. She was always wandering up and down the street talking to people or just talking away to herself. Seemed happy. Everybody knew her.

The story was she came over from the Ukraine when she was just a kid, and she was supposed to marry some guy who was waiting for her in Canada. It was all arranged like that back then. Problem was, when she got to the dock in Fort McKay—no husband. No one ever showed up to get her. That was in about nineteen twenty-something, and this poor kid was standing on the dock with her Ukrainian bride's ribbons in her hair going nuts and screaming in Ukrainian because she didn't speak any English. No one knew what to do with her, so they took her to the nuthouse. No kidding. She stayed there most of her life too. Eventually some Ukrainian folks helped her find a place to stay—but by then she was old. Well anyway, that's the story.

I took the photos in black and white and planned to paint them like that too. I was thinking about that movie *Night and Fog* and how it was mostly black and white, so when there was anything in colour you knew it was important. For the photo of Mary Christmas, when I painted her I would paint her lips and cheeks red.

I took a photo of the Odeon Theatre. *Fahrenheit 451* was playing. It was directed by Francis Truffaut but because some of the lights on the marquee were burned out it said "directed by –ranci-T---f-a-t" Ha. I took a photo of the brass bells in the steeple of Knox United Church, and I took a photo of the park across from the church with the old chestnut tree.

I took a whole series of photos of the Lorna Doone Tea Room. The Doone from the inside, the Doone from the outside, the Doone dog—classic. Nakina was with me that day—a rare event that spring. I took a shot of Nakina inside the Doone, and then I went outside when she was eating and took a shot of her through the window. The lights of the neon sign made her face green.

She didn't know I was taking the picture. She was looking straight ahead and had this faraway look on her face. Nakina always had attitude—always ready with a smart-ass remark or a joke, but that day I saw something different. That day she looked serious—maybe angry. When I went back in she was drinking a Coke and talking to the waitress, who bounced her cig between her lips as she talked. Talent.

A Coke and a smoke at the Doone. I took that shot too and I thought I would paint the lit end of the cigarette red.

"So what are you going to do with the photos?" Nakina asked.

"I told you."

"Paint them?"

"Yeah."

"So why do you have to paint them when you have the photos."

"Come on Nakina."

"Seriously. Seems like a waste of time if you already have the photos."

"I need the photos to remember the details when I…never mind."

"So, am I getting an invitation to the opening night?" she asked.

"No." I was getting angry with Nakina but I didn't really know why. I felt she was making fun of me because I was pretending to be an artist. And she was right. I was just messing around. I didn't know what I was doing.

"So what *are* you going to call your big show?" She asked.

"I don't know."

"No, really."

"Piss off!"

"Piss off. Nice. That'll look good on the poster."

"Very funny."

"Seriously, what will you call it?"

I thought for a few minutes, "Sixty-eight. Get it, from nineteen sixty-eight—the year I took the photos."

"Don't call it that."

"Why?"

"Just don't, OK."

I took another bite of my burger. "What's wrong with sixty-eight?"

"Leave it, Molly." I looked over at Nakina and could see she was getting upset.

"What's your problem?"

She was silent for a few minutes, head down looking at her plate, then she quietly said, "That was my number."

"What number?"

"In the residential school. They gave us numbers. Not names—just numbers. I was sixty-eight."

That summer Nakina came with us to our camp at Loon Lake. The camp was a couple of hours out of town on the west side of the lake. There were a lot of camps on East Loon but ours was on the far end with bush on either side. We drove to the end of the Loon Road and hauled all our food and supplies about ten minutes down a narrow path. My grandpa built the camp in 1904, and in those days, before the highway went in, they came out to the camp on the train.

Nakina and I slept in the shed near the tracks and every night at 11:30, when the Canadian rolled past, we'd sit up and watch the lights of the passenger cars flicker by.

"I'm going on that train some day." I was leaning on the windowsill trying to see the people in the cars.

"Where to?"

"Anywhere. Out of here. Think about it, you go to bed in Ontario and wake up in Manitoba or Quebec."

"And then what?"

"I don't know. It would be different that's all. Do you think that's the one?"

"What one?"

"The train in your dream. The train that brought you here."

"I dunno. Maybe."

———◆———

Every day at the lake that summer was perfect. In the morning after breakfast we would put on our bathing suits and head down to the dock. We swam and rowed around in the little rowboat called the Little Tink that my dad built for my mom. Some days we walked down the train tracks to East Loon to get candy from Hans Hogan's store, and on the walk back we'd pick pails of wild strawberries that Mom made into jam. We swam until we had elephant skin and fished off the dock using worms we found under the rocks.

One day Dad and I were splitting wood and Nakina asked if she could help. Dad showed her how to set the piece of wood she was going to split on the chopping block and stand with her feet apart. He showed her how to set the blade of the axe where she was going to make her cut and to check for knots, which could be hard to split. He showed her how to raise the axe slowly over her head, sliding one hand further along the handle and bringing it down In one fast smooth move onto the centre of the wood. She messed up a bit at first but once she got the hang of it she was pretty good.

Before supper Mom and Dad came down to the lake for a swim, and while they sat on the dock drying off we listened to them talk. Mom said when she was a kid they'd sit on the dock and listen to music from Captain Nobel's camp. He was famous. Invented some kind of gas mask I think and he had this grand piano at his camp. Don't know how it got there—maybe they took it over on a boat. Mom said sometimes his buddy Robert Flaherty visited him. Flaherty was the very first documentary filmmaker. He went up to the Arctic and shot the film *Nanook of the North*. Flaherty played violin and Captain Nobel played piano, and all the folks on the lake would sit on their docks under the moonlight listening to their music.

Sometimes after supper Dad built a bonfire, and we roasted marshmallows and watched fireflies flit like Christmas lights in the trees. If it was raining we stayed inside and Dad would put a good fire in the fireplace. Mom and Dad and Nakina played board games or cribbage, and I sat by the fire and read. I'd brought a pile of art books with me from the library. It was the best summer. Until the end.

It was our last day at camp and Nakina and I had been rowing along the shoreline in the Little Tink. We'd rowed across to East Loon because I wanted to show Nakina where Sheila Burnford lived.

"Look, there she is on her dock."

"So who is she?" Nakina asked.

"A writer. Did you ever read *The Incredible Journey*?"

"No."

"I'll lend you my copy. It's about two dogs and a cat that get separated from their owners and they cross the country to find their way home."

"And that's her?"

"Yeah." I rowed a bit closer to the dock and we could see an older woman sitting in a chair on the dock reading.

"They made a movie of it," I said.

"Of what?"

"*The Incredible Journey*. It was a movie."

Nakina was dragging her hand in the water making patterns as I rowed. I put down the oars and waved to Mrs. Burnford. She waved back.

I rowed to the far end of the lake, past the girls' camp, and then along the West Loon shore. I loved the squeaking sound the oars made in the oarlocks when I raised the paddles. We were passing a neighbour's dock and Nakina and I were talking about what we were going to do when we got back to town. She stopped talking in the middle of a sentence and when I looked up I saw she had that spacey look she got just before a seizure.

"Nakina?"

She didn't answer, so I turned the boat around and started rowing towards the closest dock, but it was too late. First she went stiff, then she started thrashing around, and before I could grab her she fell out of the boat. Mr. Ellis and his son were in front of their camp, and they both jumped in the lake and swam out to us. Mr. Ellis got Nakina's head above water but she was kicking and thrashing so hard I thought she'd take him under with her. It took two of them to get her to their dock and by that time a crowd had gathered. They laid her on the grass in front of their camp and someone ran down to the far end of the lake to get my mom and dad.

Dad drove Nakina back to our camp and put her on the couch. I sat by the fireplace watching her sleep, and I could see Mom and Dad talking outside on the dock. I couldn't hear what they were saying, but I knew it wasn't good.

Nakina woke up early in the afternoon and had a big lunch, and even though we weren't supposed to go home until the next day, Mom and Dad closed the camp and we headed into town that night.

———◈———

When it came to clothes Nakina and I were like real sisters—ready to rip each other's throats out. Nakina was big on clothes. I wasn't. The great divide. She went in for lipstick and miniskirts and backcombed hair, and I went for no make-up, patched jeans and bare feet.

"God Molly, throw this blouse out."

"You don't have to wear it."

"I wouldn't wear it; I'm not a lumberjack."

"Lumberjack blouse. Good one," I said.

"Seriously, you could make an effort. It wouldn't kill you."

"What for?"

"To look good," she said.

"For who?"

"For anyone."

"Shut up."

"No, you shut up."

"I hate your face pretty much."

"No, I hate your face pretty much."

We always ended our arguments with the Fort McKay official greeting "I hate your face pretty much." It meant a lot of things, like "Hi" or "See you later" or "Go to hell." It was versatile.

It was OK for Nakina to talk about clothes. She looked good in everything. She had it all—straight black hair she didn't have to iron every night. Dark skin—no blotchy freckles. She had high cheekbones, a long narrow face and a thin straight nose that made her look real classy. She was built too and she knew it.

Jeans were good enough for me. They hid my skinny legs and boney knees and the lumberjack shirt hid my flat chest. Each to her own.

One day after school we were in Portland's Ladies Wear, the snootiest store in town, and Nakina wanted to try on a fur coat. A fur coat, for christ's sake. I just had to get out of there. The owner, Mr. Portland, was about to throw us out because of that whole unwritten law about not being allowed in the store if you're an Indian. He was doing that crossed arms thing, and Nakina waltzed in and said "I'd like to try…" She stopped speaking and put her head down for a moment, then looked up and said, "try on this fur coat please."

I was worried. Nakina was getting these pauses between her words that happen just before she has a seizure. So I said we'd better go. Thought if I could get some food into her—we hadn't had lunch—well, that was what I thought so I said let's go to the Lorna Doone.

"Order me a burger," she said. "I'll be there in a minute." Mr. Portland gave her the coat to try on but he didn't look happy. I didn't want to go but she gave me *the look,* the raised eyebrow look that said don't mess with me, so I went.

———————◆———————

"Coney dog and burger please. And two Cokes." Stavros the cook was listening to the radio full blast. He was from Greece and couldn't speak much English so he listened to the radio and repeated everything he heard. It was weird but it worked for Stavros — his English was getting better.

Coming back to the table with the tray I could see Nakina coming out of Portland's. I put the tray down and bit into my Coney dog. There was some secret ingredient in it, and I thought maybe it was sauerkraut. I looked out the window to see what was keeping Nakina but she wasn't there. After a few minutes I looked out the window again. Nothing. I went to the door and looked down the street. Weird. I figured she'd gone back into Portland's, and I thought I'd better drag her out because her burger was getting cold.

I walked down the street towards Portland's. I crossed a laneway between the restaurant and Portland's and a cop car caught my eye. It was parked in the lane with a cop standing behind it. I don't know why I stopped. Something about the way the cop was looking at the ground. His back was to me and he was laughing and shouting at something on the ground.

I walked down the lane to the car and in the shadow behind it I saw a hand. Nakina's hand with the turquoise ring I gave her at Christmas. I wanted to run towards her and tell the cop she had epilepsy and he needed to make sure she didn't choke but I stopped. My hands pushed against the side of the car and everything went slow. Nakina's eyes were open but she couldn't see me, and her hair was spread around her head like a black halo. Her legs were spread wide and her skirt was pulled up around her waist. Then I saw the other cop lying on top of her. The cop who was standing shouted "Give'r good, Bernie."

The cop on top of Nakina let out a groan, dropped down on her and turned his head. It was Bernie Olfson. Mr. Olfson from down the street. Then everything sped up—shouting—the cops were shouting at me or each other, and Mr. Olfson was doing up his pants and the car doors slammed and they squealed back out of the alley and I ran to Nakina and pulled her skirt down and then the waitress from the Lorna Doone was standing over me saying "Christ, what happened?"

"The cops." I looked up at her and said "The cops had her on the ground and then Olfson…" I stopped, the word *raped* frozen on my lips. I looked at Nakina lying exposed and vulnerable on the gravel, then turned back to the waitress and said "She had a seizure. She has epilepsy and she had a seizure."

chapter five

Rumours were flying around school. All true. Nakina got fat and started wearing my oversized lumberjack shirts that she hated. She was pregnant. I knew that. Just like I knew she was sick the day we were at Portland's, and I walked out of the store and left her.

Nakina kept coming over to the house, but she stopped playing cards with Mom and Dad, and mostly she sat in my room, reading. We were reading *To Kill a Mockingbird* for school. Nakina was lying on the bed beside me.

"What's a chifforobe?" I asked.

"What?"

"A chifforobe. What's a chifforobe?"

"A wardrobe. You know, for hanging clothes in."

"So what's it doing in the yard?" I asked.

"What?"

"What's a chifforobe doing sitting in the yard?"

"Molly shut up. I'm trying to read."

"Doesn't make any sense. I mean why would it be just sitting out in the yard."

"Just read to yourself."

"And why would Mayella Ewell ask Tom Robinson to come into the yard and bust it up?" I knew I was pissing her off and I gave her a kick. I was trying to kick her out of her bad mood.

"Leave me alone," Nakina said.

"I mean what was she going to do with a bust-up chifforobe anyway?"

Nakina closed her book, got up quietly and said, "I'm going home."

It was weird. She wasn't angry. Usually I could really get her going and she'd tell me to fuck off, and I'd tell her to fuck off and then we'd start laughing. That day she just got up quietly and went home.

The week before Nakina disappeared we were sitting on the wharf in front of Elevator B at the mouth of the Kam River. Dad was going to pick us up in the boat and take us out to the Welcome Islands. There were some kids behind us on the tracks playing Whack-a-Rat. A Fort McKay sport. See, along the railway line behind the elevators were these rats that gorged themselves on the grain that spilled out of the boxcars. They'd swell up and get as big as beavers and waddle slowly along the tracks waiting to die. So kids would come out along the tracks with baseball bats and chase them and then…WHACK. Dead rat. Gross. I didn't think it would ever become an Olympic sport.

Nakina watched them for a while, and when the bat came down she said, "Lucky rat."

"God, Nakina!"

"Better than lying there swelling up until it dies."

My dad came along with the boat, but as soon as we got out on the lake Nakina got sick. We turned around and headed back to the dock.

Then she was gone. I didn't know where she was, and I never asked. I heard my mom and dad talking about her one night in the kitchen after I'd gone to bed but I couldn't catch what they were saying.

I missed her. Missed her like crazy. Missed her at home, missed her playing cards with mom and dad, missed her sleeping on the pullout cot in my room, missed her telling me what to do. I was so used to following Nakina that after she left I was lost. Just wandered around school in a daze looking like I'd taken a puck to the head.

I went back to being the weird, skinny, invisible kid I used to be, and I tried to fill the space with books—increased my habit to a book a day. It didn't help.

I started to hang out with Anna. Her dad worked with my dad at the mill, and our families got together at the Hoito restaurant on Sunday mornings. I liked Anna; she was a straight-ahead kid. She had something wrong with her legs so she walked with canes most of the time, which wasn't a big deal. When Nakina disappeared I started spending more time with Anna at school.

We had lunch together and joined the drama club, which

was the first club I'd ever joined. Our drama teacher, Mrs. Miller, was amazing. She wasn't just a teacher; she'd worked as a director in theatres all across the country and she was really well connected. It was because of Mrs. Miller that we had a big theatre production from out west visit our school. The play was *The Ecstasy of Rita Joe*. We didn't know much about it except that the whole school was getting the afternoon off to watch it, so that was good.

After lunch we all headed to the gym. The bleachers were pushed back, and they had set up a stage in the middle. It was about two feet high with a ramp up the left side. At the back, right-hand side there was another ramp going up to a level about a foot higher, and on this platform was a big black desk with a gavel lying on the top. I had never seen a live play before. The gym was packed with hundreds of students, but it was totally silent as soon as the play began. We sat on the floor and there was one bright light, focused on the stage. Through the main doors came about a dozen actors. They walked across the gym floor and up the ramp onto the stage and faced us. The lights in the gym dimmed and a spotlight shone on a woman standing in front of a judge, who sat behind the big desk on the higher level.

The play was about this girl, Rita Joe, who was Cree I think. Anyway, she left home on the reserve and went into town looking for work. She was in town and had no money and men were harassing her. Rita kept talking to this guy she loved and he wasn't there and you just wanted someone to…I mean her sister tried, and her father, well he missed her so much but they were far away. Too far away. And Rita couldn't get out of the city, and the policemen…. I had to leave. I got up quietly and made my way to the door. I could see Mrs. Miller looking at me. I left without my coat and by the time I got to the parking lot I was running. I kept running until I got deep into the woods at the back of the school.

Where was Nakina? Where was she?

———◈———

One morning about five months later she was back. Just like that. I was at my locker sorting through the books I needed for class and I looked up and there she was turning her lock. She had to do it a few times; I guess she'd forgotten the combination. She got her books, closed her locker and walked up to me and said "Hey Molly."

"Hey," I said.

"We got shorthand this morning?" she asked.

I said, "Yeah."

"Do we have a spare after, or history?"

"History." I said.

She said "OK" and led the way down the hall. I followed her.

I wanted to hug her and ask where the hell she'd been and what happened, but she just grabbed her books and walked past me down the hall like it was no big deal. So I followed her like it was no big deal.

She looked the same when she came back but something had changed. It was like that film *Invasion of the Body Snatchers*, where people look the same but inside they're empty pod people. It was like that with Nakina. People thought it was her but I knew it wasn't. Not really. At first she started coming home with me again, and Mom and

Dad acted like nothing had happened, and I told myself that maybe nothing had and everything was the same. But I knew it wasn't.

She was in a new foster home. Said the Dekkers had kicked her out, which was strange because they seemed like really nice people. She was living with the school janitor, Mr. Starke, and his wife and she said it was OK. I thought it was creepy. He was creepy with his white shoes and gold chains on his hairy chest and always stinking of Brut aftershave and the disinfectant he used to scrub the floors. Nakina said he was OK. Said they knew how to have a good time. She stopped coming home with me after a while, and I got the feeling that she didn't think my family knew how to have a good time. I felt hurt, but I wasn't sure why.

It was small things I noticed at first. Like her laugh. She used to crack me up with her deep belly laugh. She didn't laugh much any more and when she did I always felt like the joke was on me. I began to see things. She wore a lot of make-up at school. I noticed she had new jewelry and the chain around her neck looked like real gold. She didn't wear the dime store turquoise ring I gave her anymore.

She came for Easter dinner. Hadn't been over for ages and it felt good to have her back.

"Molly, can you set the table?"

"I'm peeling the potatoes. Nakina can do it."

"Get Nakina to finish the potatoes. She does a better job than you." Mom took her apron off and put her hand on my shoulder. "There's no potato left when you peel them."

"Thanks a lot." I handed the paring knife to Nakina.

"Fork on the left, Molly," Mom said.

Mom made a fantastic turkey dinner and Nakina raved

about the apple pie and after dinner they played cribbage. Dad got out the slide projector and screen, and I teased him about showing us hundreds of pictures of his racing boats, but we looked at slides of Loon Lake and laughed about how short and goofy we were. Pictures of me and Nakina rowing the Little Tink across the lake, sitting around the bonfire at night roasting marshmallows, carrying the water pail back from the well.

I was watching the slides and thinking maybe I was wrong—maybe nothing had changed. I was thinking maybe the problem was me. Then Dad took the picture.

"Come on girls let's get a picture of you two. You've grown a foot since last summer." It was true. I had grown up a foot but not out. I was tall and skinny and flat chested and awkward, and I was wishing my dad would just put the camera away.

"Come on Nakina, get over there with Molly in front of the chair…perfect. OK, everyone say 'cheese.'" We were laughing and had our arms around each other and it felt like it used to. But a week later when the photos came back I saw it.

I looked about ten years old—skinny as a rail with no hips or breasts. I looked like a little girl. Nakina looked like a woman. Sophisticated. She was wearing a sleeveless dress and had her hair pulled back in a bun.

I looked at the photo for a long time, and then I went to my room and crawled under the blankets and let the waterworks roll. I don't know if I was crying because I was ashamed of how I looked, or because I realized how Nakina saw me—how everyone saw me. No wonder she didn't want to hang out with me anymore.

After that Nakina took some different classes and didn't eat with me in the cafeteria. We started to drift apart.

chapter six

"You look like you're wearing fishnet stockings."

"Fuck off."

"You fuck off."

Anna was in a wheelchair after her operation and her legs were a crisscross of scars.

"Let's celebrate."

"Celebrate what?"

"I don't know. You getting sprung from the hospital," I said. "Let's take the day off and hang out down at the river."

We went down to the Kam River with a pack of smokes and a bottle of 772B. You had to fill out these forms in the liquor store and I'd memorized the cheapest brew, 772B—Old Sailor Sherry. We knew how to have a good time.

"What if a train comes?"

I was pulling Anna's wheelchair backwards over the tracks. "It won't," I said.

"How do you know?"

"Two trains a day. One in the morning and the other about ten at night."

"You sure?"

"Have I ever been wrong before?" I said.

"I'm dead."

"Seriously. They hardly use these tracks since the elevators closed."

"Christ Molly, go easy. Do you want me to end up back in hospital?"

"Sorry. Just one more track and we're home free. Don't drop the wine."

"You're shaking me out of my freakin chair and all you care about is the wine."

"Right," I said, "hold on to the wine."

When we got down to the waterfront I had two brilliant ideas. The first was that Anna should put the brakes on her chair because the wharf was on an angle and if she rolled into the Kam I would be in deep shit. The second idea came when I was lying on my back looking up at Sask Wheat Pool Number 7. We had just polished off half a bottle of 772B and everything had a rosy glow.

"Hey, look up there," I said.

"Where."

"Top of the elevator."

"Yeah. So what?" she asked.

"The square building on top."

"Yeah."

"What's that?" I asked.

"That's the electrician's office. My uncle used to be the electrician and that was his office. He took me up one day—very cool."

"No shit. How'd you get up there? The fire escape?"

"No idiot. There was an elevator."

"An elevator in an elevator! Good one! You know, this place has been closed down for a few years."

"Yeah. So?"

"So that office is empty."

"Yeah. So what."

"So it's perfect," I said.

"Perfect for what?"

"A studio," I said.

"What?"

"A painting studio. Lots of windows, good light."

"Lay off the Old Sailors," Anna said.

"Philistine."

"Asshole."

"I hate your face pretty much."

I got up and walked toward the rusted ladder that went up the side of the elevator. Worth a try. I began to climb.

Near the top some screws that secured the ladder to the concrete had come loose.

I hung on tight but my legs started vibrating with the ladder. Not good. I kept going and at the top stepped onto a flat gravel roof and walked toward the door of the wooden building. I figured it would be locked but it wasn't. Inside was a long room about six times the length of our house. There were windows all along one side—the side that looked out to the Kam. There was a lot of crap on the floor—pieces of wood, broken furniture, some weird electrical stuff—but it wasn't as bad as I thought it would be. Along the front of the room under the windows was a long workbench. I cleared some of it off, pushing all the stuff into a metal garbage can.

I found a stool upside down under some wood and pulled it out, dusted it off and pulled it up to the workbench. Not bad. Not bad at all.

After a bit I climbed back down and bummed a Cameo menthol off Anna.

"So?" she asked.

"So what?"

"What's it like up there?"

"Great. I'm moving in."

"Oh yeah. Penthouse apartment."

"Yeah. Gonna help me move in?" I asked.

"Funny."

"No, seriously."

We headed back to my place, bopping over three sets of tracks, and I loaded a cardboard box of paint, brushes and canvases onto Anna's lap.

"You're better than a little red wagon."

"You owe me big for this. This shit is heavy you know."

We had more trouble getting back across the tracks this time. Might have had something to do with the Old Sailor's. It took about four trips up the ladder to move my stuff in. There were still things I needed but I figured if I brought a bit each day I'd soon have the place set up nice.

I spent most of that fall in my studio. Anna's mom worked in a print shop and she made business cards for me:

Molly Bell, Artist
Sask Pool 7 Studio

After school and on the weekends I'd head over to Sask Pool 7. I brought a few things every day and after about a month I had it set up the way I wanted it. Took an old rag and cleaned the windows and when I was done the light in the room was amazing. I set up an easel in the corner and put my paints and brushes on the workbench. Along the workbench I laid out the photos I had taken the year before. I was working on the one I'd taken of Nakina sitting in the restaurant. I had a few bad starts and was getting frustrated. I couldn't get her head right, the way she was leaning forward with her face in profile.

I thought about the day I took the photos—back when Nakina and I hung out all the time and fought like sisters. I missed her. I wanted to show her my studio. I wanted to talk to her and find out what she was thinking the day I took that photo. Why did she look so serious? Was she angry? Angry with me for taking the photos?

Was she angry with me now? Is that why she drifted away? I kept painting but couldn't get her face right and I was getting pissed off with myself for being such a shitty painter. Finally I gave up and sat down staring at the photo. She seemed so far away.

Some days I'd stop painting and look down the Kam River out onto Lake Superior, out to the Stone Man. I could see boats, mostly small boats—not many grain boats anymore. I could see deer out on Mission Island and sometimes, when bigger boats came down the river, I got to see the swing bridge lift to let them through. When I climbed down the ladder at night the sun was setting and the light turned the granite cliffs of the mountains to gold.

I loved my studio. When I was painting I lost all track of time and the more I worked the more I realized how much I had to learn. I began to think seriously about going to art school. I'd been reading information about the Nova Scotia College of Art and Design—sculpture, ceramics, painting, art history. It all sounded good.

By November it was getting too cold to work without heat so I had to shut down Sask Pool 7. I wrapped my canvases up in heavy black plastic and tied rope around them. It took hours to lower them all down to the wharf.

It was almost dark when I came down. Needed gloves 'cause the cold metal railings of the ladder froze my fingers. I stayed on the wharf until the last bit of sunlight was gone. There was a full moon. A low yellow moon reflecting off the Kam.

I set up the easel in my bedroom but it was wasn't the same. My room was too small and dark. I missed my studio.

Anna was hanging out in my bedroom with me that afternoon. "What's that one?" she asked.

"It's Nakina at the Doone."

"Doesn't look like her."

"Thanks."

"Just saying."

"It's a work in progress," I said.

"What's this?" Anna picked up a book from my desk.

"Hieronymus Bosch," I said.

She opened the book and looked at a double spread of twisted naked bodies writhing in flames. "Holy shit," she said, "this guy must have been smoking some weird stuff."

"That's *The Garden of Earthly Delights*. It's a moral statement—don't do bad stuff or the devil will get you."

She looked back at the picture of Nakina. "So what's up with Nakina anyway?" Anna asked.

"What do you mean?"

"Haven't seen her around for a while."

"So…"

"So you guys used to do everything together. You were like Siamese twins."

"Yeah."

"So what happened?"

"Why don't you ask her?"

When Anna left I moved my paints and easel into the basement. It was cold and damp down there, and there was no light except from one bulb that hung beside the furnace, but at least it was a place I could work in peace. A space of my own.

I spent most of the winter alone in the basement, painting. I thought I was making progress, but when I stood back and looked at what I'd created, I could see it was all crap.

chapter seven

'd pretty much given up on Nakina that spring when I found her waiting for me at my locker on the last day of school.

I ignored her. Didn't want to make the first move.

She leaned against my locker and said, "Got a job."

"Yeah."

"Yeah," Nakina said.

"So."

"So, I'm going to Rocky Lake."

"Rocky Lake?" I asked.

"North of Pickle Lake."

"Where the hell is Pickle Lake?" I asked.

"North of Pine River."

"Where the hell is…"

"Molly! Get an atlas!"

"So what's the deal?"

"I'm working in the clinic there."

"Oh yeah. Put all your nursing training to good use?"

"Very funny. I'm the office assistant. Helping the nurse."

"So, how'd you get the job?"

"Mitch, at the Friendship Centre. He heard they were looking for someone and he set it up for me."

"Hey Anishinaabe, good on ya. Do you get to wear a little white nurse's dress?"

"I hate your face pretty much," she said.

"Come for dinner. You can tell Mom and Dad all about it."

Nakina came home with me that night and Mom came downstairs to talk to her. That was a big thing because Mom had been spending more and more time in bed. "How will you get up there?" Mom asked.

"Plane. I take the bus to Pickle Lake then I fly into Rocky Lake."

"How long will you be there?"

"Till the end of August. I'll be back for school."

"And what will you be doing?" Mom asked.

"Not too sure. Mitch said I'd be helping out the nurse in the clinic. Office stuff—filing, typing, that sort of thing."

Before Nakina left I gave her two gifts— a fancy box of writing paper covered with blue flowers and a camera with eight rolls of film.

"What's with the camera? You think I'm going up there as a tourist?"

"No. I just thought. You know. You might be able to record what it's like up there—like the photos I took on First Avenue last year."

"Yeah. Maybe."

Nakina sent a few short letters that summer. The first ones were on the blue flower stationary I gave her.

July 2, 1970
Hey white girl,

Thanks for the writing paper. The trip up here was OK, but the bus ride was gross. Some kid in the seat behind me threw up just after we left town so the bus stank the whole way up to Pickle Lake. And the roads are crazy—really rough and bumpy so I felt like puking too by the time we got here.

The bus was late getting into town so I don't fly out till tomorrow morning. I stayed in a motel and man oh man there was some party going on. A bunch of guys from the mine were in town and they'd just got paid, so there was a lot of drinking. Well, there was supposed to be some women coming into town so they organized this dance in the bar—but the women didn't show up. So it's just the guys. And they're drunk, and there's music—so some of the guys start waltzing together, and then this one guy cuts in on another guy's "lady" and they all start fighting. It was pretty funny. I could hear the whole thing through the wall of my room cause the walls are as thin as paper.

So, anyway, I'm going to mail this in the morning before I fly out. Once I get to Rocky Lake I don't know how long it will take for mail to get to you.

Nakina

July 3, 1970
Hey Molly,

*The plane trip up here was amazing! I flew in a
Cessna. Ask your dad what that is, he'll know. It's really
small and there was just the pilot, and me and Monique
the nurse I'm going to be working with. She is really
nice. She's from Trinidad. Isn't that cool.*

*Anyway when we were up in the air you could see for
hundreds of miles. Boy, are there ever a lot of lakes. And
trees. I was worried about landing because I thought
we might hit the water pretty rough, but you could
hardly tell when the pontoons hit the water. There is a
big government dock here where we got off the plane
and then Monique and I went up to the clinic and got
unpacked.*

*I've got a room to myself and then we share a little
kitchen with a stove and a fridge. We've got a TV set, but
you can't get any reception here.*

Nakina

July 8, 1970

*So Molly, did you get my letters? When are you going
to write to me? I've been really busy. As soon as we
got here there were people waiting to see the nurse so I
didn't have much time to figure out what I'm supposed
to do. I'm in charge of the patient files, and I book the
appointments, but really people just come in when they*

want to see the nurse. Most of the things aren't serious, just colds, and sprained ankles and stuff like that. There are a few old people who have diabetes and they come in for their insulin shots. Anyway, got to run, lots of work to do. Write!

Nakina

I was really glad to get letters from Nakina. Things at home weren't great. Mom spent more and more time in bed, and when she was up she was quiet and sad. I kept telling Dad that if we went to camp it would cheer her up, but Mom said she didn't want to go. Anna and her family were away for the summer, staying with some relatives in Minnesota. I spent most of my time in Sask Pool 7. I'd set up my studio again and was glad to get out of the house.

I painted and read books about painting and sketching and perspective. I told Nakina what I was learning in my letters, but it wasn't the same as having her around to hang out with.

July 15, 1970
Hey Molly,

I got your package and letter. Thanks for the cookies. They're not as good as the ones your mom bakes, but they tasted OK.

Sounds like your summer is pretty boring. I hope you'll get to go to Loon Lake when your mom is feeling better.

Things here are good. At night after work Monique and I go down to the dock and wait for the fishing boats to come in. They catch a lot of pickerel here. We gut them and cook them over an open fire out on the beach. Last night I had breaded pickerel cheeks—really good.

Oh, guess what! Yesterday I helped deliver a baby. Her name is Sarah. Monique let me help clean her up and I wrapped her in a blanket and gave her to her mom. It was pretty cool.

Nakina

July 18, 1970
Dear Molly,

Thanks for the letter. Those goofy cartoons you drew all over it were pretty funny. I have to tell you about the naming ceremony. Remember I told you that I helped Monique deliver a baby. Sarah. Well, that is her English name, but she gets an Ojibwe name too.

So here's how it works. Sarah's mom and dad went to Moses, he's a shaman, and gave him a gift of tobacco, then they asked him to name their baby. After that Moses went away for a few days to find a name. Sometimes he prays for a name, and sometimes it comes in a dream.

When he has the name there's a ceremony, and that happened today. Two drummers led everyone along the road to the field beside the sweat lodge. They burned tobacco for an offering.

Then Moses said the baby's name out loud, and then we all said her new name out loud. It was Memengwaa. It means butterfly. Lillian was carrying Memengwaa in *a tikinagan, that's a cradleboard, and Moses said it was the same cradleboard her mom and grandmother were carried in. It has a wooden frame and it's got beautiful beading down the front.*

After the ceremony there was a big feast and I ate so much I could hardly move. There are about sixty-five people living here. Did I tell you that before? Pretty small compared to Fort McKay.

Nakina

I read Nakina's letter out loud to Mom and Dad that night and they said it sounded like she was learning a lot. Mom told me her friend Martha from up north carried her baby in a tikinagan when she worked on her trapline. I wondered if Nakina was taking any photographs. I wanted to see what Rocky Lake looked like.

July 25, 1970
Hi Molly,

Things get pretty crazy up here at night. It's not a dry reserve so there's lots of drinking. Oh did I tell you that Monique has a boyfriend in Toronto? His name is Miley and he is a jazz musician. He plays saxophone.

Anyway, at night Monique locks the doors of the clinic. We even have metal bars on the windows. Need them too. People try to get in to get drugs. I don't go out at night.

Nakina

July 27, 1970
Boozhoo Molly,

Guess what. I'm learning to speak Ojibwe, or re-learning I guess—they wouldn't let me speak it at the residential school so I forgot a lot. Moses started to teach me, and now Dora, who everyone calls Auntie, is teaching me. She comes every day to the clinic for her insulin shot. I'm learning pretty fast. I asked Auntie to teach me how to swear but she just laughed. Anyway, miigwech for the package. You're getting to be a good cook. Monique loved the ginger cake and wants you to send some more!

I can't believe it is nearly the end of July already. It will be hard to come home because I really like it here. But there are times, like late at night when there is a lot of drinking and fighting when I wish I were back home where it was safe.

Nakina

Dad and I finally persuaded Mom to go to Loon Lake, and as soon as we got there she seemed to feel better. Dad and I painted the rowboat and mom made jam from the wild raspberries we picked along the tracks. We'd sit out on the dock at night talking or just listening to the loons cry out to each other across the lake.

There were two letters waiting for me when I got back from Loon Lake. Nakina's life at Rocky Lake sounded exciting and interesting. Made my life seem boring. Once we got back from camp Mom settled back into her moods again and I spent most of the time in my studio painting. I liked painting, but it was lonely.

July 30, 1970
Dear Molly,

Happy Birthday! I didn't forget. I have a present for you but you won't get it till I get back. Thanks for the letter and the extra film. I've been taking a lot of photos. The sunsets here are really beautiful.

Sometimes being up here reminds me of being at Loon Lake with you guys. Last week I went out with Lillian, the girl that had the baby, and Dora, and we picked blueberries. Lillian taught me how to make blueberry bannock. It's really good and simple to make too. I'll show you when I get back. When we were cooking Lillian told me that she had gone to residential school too. Not St. Mary's but one near Kenora. I think it messed her up, but she doesn't say much about it.

Anyway, I'm really busy every day. As soon as we get up there are people at the door waiting to see Monique. Last week a guy got shot—I think it was a hunting accident. Anyway they had to fly him out to the hospital at Sioux Lookout. I had to call for the plane on the shortwave radio. I'm learning a lot.

Nakina

August 6, 1970
Molly,

Sorry about the paper, I ran out of writing paper, and there's nothing to write on here except this paper towel. Supplies are hard to get and we're always running out of stuff. Especially drugs. Remember I told you about Moses the shaman? Well, after Sarah's naming ceremony I asked him if I could have a name. Moses said that I was probably given a name when I was born but since there is no one who remembers it Moses said he would give me a new name. I gave him tobacco, as a gift, and now I have to wait for him to find my name.

Oh, and guess what. Auntie made me a jingle dress. The top is embroidered with red and green ribbons and below the waist there's five rows of tin jingles in a V pattern. She is going to teach me to dance. I'll show you when I get back.

Nakina

August 15, 1970

Molly, something really sad happened. You know I told you about Moses. Well, he died. He was really old, and Monique said he had a bad heart.

I learned a lot from him and he said I could call him Mishomis, which means Grandfather. I miss him.

Nakina

Aug. 17, 1970
Boozhoo Molly,

*I wish you were here. This was a really hard week.
Remember I told you about Lillian, she had a baby just
after I got here. Well Lillian likes to drink, and a bunch
of people came into town, and Lillian went on a bender.
When Monique found out she sent me over to her place
to make sure the baby was OK. I went into her place
and no one was there—but it smelled bad. I was about
to leave when I saw all these flies over by the window, so
I went over and the baby was lying there covered in shit
and flies. She wasn't even crying. I grabbed a blanket
and wrapped her up and ran back to the clinic.*

*They had to fly her out to the hospital in Sioux
Lookout that night. Lillian didn't show up for another
two days so she didn't even know her kid was gone.*

Well, that's all from me.

Nakina

A week later Nakina showed up at our door, grinning. "Hey
white girl."

"Hey Anishinaabe" I said.

"So what's for dinner?" She was smiling but she looked
like hell.

"You didn't tell me you were coming back," I said.

"Couldn't. Clinic burned down. They flew us out
yesterday."

Nakina came in and when my mom saw her she made
her strip down and have a bath. Mom put her clothes in the

wash because they still smelled like smoke and she told me to find something for her to wear. Mom cooked a roast beef for dinner, even though it wasn't Sunday. It was good to see Mom up and out of bed and acting like her old self again. Nakina always brought a spark of life into the house.

That night in my room when we were getting ready for bed I asked Nakina if Moses had given her a name before he died.

"Waawaashkeshi."

"What's it mean?"

"Deer. White-tailed deer."

"Not dear, like Dear Nakina, how are you, I am fine," I said.

"And there was a sweat lodge ceremony,"

"Like Kanga's sauna?"

"No, idiot."

"So what was it like?"

"It's hard to describe. The sweat lodge wasn't big—not big enough to stand up in. There was an opening that faced east and a big fire pit outside the entrance. That's where they heat the stones. And the day before the sweat I had to fast. I could drink water, but I couldn't eat all day, and I had to think about my question."

"Question?"

"What I wanted to ask in the sweat lodge."

"So what was your question?"

Nakina turned away from me and was quiet. I thought maybe I shouldn't have asked.

"So…Waawaashkeshi," I said.

"Yeah."

"I like it."

"So did you paint these?" Nakina was looking at the paintings I had done of First Avenue.

"Yeah, what do you think?"

"Not bad for a white person."

"Seriously."

"They're good. What's this one?" she asked.

"The Lorna Doone. Remember that day I took all the photos.

"No."

"Yes you do. You told me I was an idiot.'

"I always tell you you're an idiot. I look green."

"Neon lights."

"Is it finished?"

"That one? No. It's hard to get the reflection in the glass. Hey?"

"What."

"You never said what happened to the baby that was sick," I said.

"She died."

"Died?"

"Yeah." Nakina spoke so quietly I could hardly hear her. "They flew her to the hospital in Sioux Lookout, but she was too dehydrated."

I wanted to ask Nakina more but I could tell she was upset. I wanted to find some words to let her know I was sorry but I didn't know what to say.

"I took pictures," she said.

"In Rocky Lake?"

"Six rolls and there is one still in the camera."

"We can take the film in tomorrow and get it developed."

"Sure."

"Nakina?" I asked.

"Yeah?"

"What happened? With the fire?"

"Problem with the wiring. Good thing it happened during the day. We got out right away. Everyone helped to put it out—got buckets of water from the lake but it was no use. At least we kept it from spreading."

"And then you came back."

"Had to. No place to live. Monique went back to Toronto."

"Will they build another clinic?"

"Don't know. Probably not. It would take a lot of money."

———————————

When the pictures came back we had a special dinner. Dad cooked pickerel on the barbeque just for Nakina and Mom made ginger cake for dessert. Nakina gave me my birthday present, a small basket woven with porcupine quills that Dora had made.

"OK, this photo is down at the dock. The fishing boats are coming in. And that's the pickerel I caught." Nakina showed us a photo of her standing on the dock grinning from ear to ear and holding a small fish in the air. "In this one they're gutting the fish and see the fire in the background?"

"Yeah?"

"We fried up the fish right there, in a cast iron frying pan."

"Who's that standing beside you?" I asked, looking at the face of an old man.

"That's Moses. He taught me how to fish. And that's

Monique," she said, showing us a photo of a tall black woman standing in the doorway of the clinic. "And this is my favourite," she said, showing us a photo of a bright red sunset taken from a canoe.

"Will you go back?" I asked.

"I hope so."

Nakina took the photos and tucked them carefully into a shoebox my mom gave her, along with the letters. She had saved every one I'd sent her that summer.

chapter eight

Nakina stayed at our place till school started. I wanted her to move in with us, and I think Mom and Dad wanted that too, but Social Services came knocking. Her worker had placed her with Mr. Starke, the janitor from our school, so she had to go back and live with him and his wife again. She didn't want to and I didn't blame her. He was a real creep, but Nakina didn't have a choice, so she packed up and moved back in with them.

At lunch she hung out with Anna and me, and sometimes we all went to the Doone after school. I started taking photos again. Nakina still had the camera I gave her when she went up to Rocky Lake and sometimes we went out to take pictures together.

I took a photo of an old guy unloading crates of carrots and corn at the farmer's market early in the morning. I went back to my old ballet studio and took photos of Mrs. Palmer with her short fat legs and a cigarette balanced between her thick fingers, telling the girls to plié, down two three, up two three. And all the little girls in their pink tutus and white tights. I took photos of their arms raised in graceful circles above their heads and close-ups of their fingers outstretched like the tips of swans' wings.

Nakina took photos of people sitting on park benches and the window of the Woolworths store. One afternoon Dad took us out in the boat, and I brought my camera and took photos of Dad at the back of the boat with his hand on the throttle. You could see the silhouette of the Sleeping Giant behind him. I took a photo of Nakina from behind with her hair blowing in the wind, and just after I took that photo she turned around and gave me a silly grin and I took that shot too.

I was beginning to think Nakina's summer up north had fixed things between us. We were spending more time together, and we started going to the Friday night dances at the Native Friendship Centre in North Fort. Dad drove us over and we'd hang out in the main hall drinking pop and eating sandwiches and listening to music. As soon as we walked in guys would pull Nakina on to the dance floor and she'd be dancing the whole night. I was happy to sit on the bench against the wall and watch the fun. I made a few friends and hung out with Marcel, a guy who was going to Lakehead, and we'd talk about politics and philosophy, which was better than dancing. Mitch Dancau ran the Centre and was always there keeping an eye on things and getting to know all the kids. He was like the grandfather of the Friendship Centre.

Things seemed good, but in November Nakina stopped going to the dances. Said it had something to do with her foster family, but she wouldn't tell me more. I could feel her sliding away again.

In early December I got called to the office. The principal just wanted to tell me they were putting my name in for an art scholarship. Nice. When I came out Nakina was sitting outside. "Hey, what's up?" I asked.

"Don't know. What are you doing…" Nakina didn't finish. Two police officers came into the office and spoke to the secretary. She buzzed for the principal and when he came out he called Nakina into his office. The police officers followed. I wanted to hang around to see what was happening, but the school secretary told me to go back to class. Later that day when I went to my locker I saw that Nakina's was wide open and empty. She was gone.

That night I got my dad to drive me to Mr. Starke's house. Dad knew where he lived because he'd driven Nakina home before. I knocked at the door but no one answered. I knew they were home because there was loud music playing. I rang the bell a few more times. Finally Mrs. Starke answered. She was holding a beer in one hand and looked like she'd had a few already. I could see some people down the hallway and in the living room.

"Is Nakina here?"

"She is not."

"Do you know where she is?"

"Don't know, don't care. She won't be coming back here is all I know."

"Well, do you…"

"Look honey, why don't you just get on home."

Just then Mr. Starke came to the door. He saw my dad waiting in the car and he told his wife to go back inside.

"Your friend doesn't live here anymore."

"Where is she?"

"I got nothing to say. Go on home.

At school kids were talking. The rumour was there was five hundred dollars missing from the office—money the students had raised for the trip to Quebec. Mr. Starke said he found it in Nakina's bedroom.

I didn't get it. Everyone knew Mr. Starke was a jerk. Why didn't Nakina just tell the police the truth? I was worried but Anna told me not to get my knickers in a twist. Said it would all get sorted out and Nakina would get in touch when she was good and ready.

I retreated to my basement studio and started a new painting. I took the painting of Nakina off the easel and laid it against the concrete wall. I put up a fresh canvas and began to paint the waitress from the Lorna Doone with a cigarette balanced between her lips.

<hr/>

By December I had three canvases done. The one of the clock tower wasn't bad. Like all the paintings it was mainly black and white, but the hands of the clock were red. I was happy with the one of the dance class but I was having a hard time with the one of Nakina in the Lorna Doone. I kept messing up her face and painting over it. And the reflection on the glass from the neon lights was hard to get. I wasn't happy with it but I thought it would have to do. I decided to give it to Nakina. Maybe I just needed a reason to go looking for her. Only problem was I didn't know where she lived. I went to the office and gave Mrs. Balcomino, the school secretary, the third degree.

"Sorry, you know I can't give out personal information."

"It's not for me, it's for my parents. They want to invite her for Christmas dinner. They said you'd understand and you wouldn't want her to spend Christmas alone."

Bingo—that did the trick. I walked out of the office with "last known address," 761 Simpson Avenue, Fort McKay South.

I finished the painting and wrapped it up in brown paper. Got it done in time for Christmas Eve, which seemed like a good time to give her the gift. I didn't tell Mom and Dad about my plans, maybe because I wasn't sure I was doing the right thing.

"Molly, you ready?" Mom asked. "We're heading over to Uncle Harry's in an hour."

"Not going."

"Why not?"

"I'm going to hang out with Nakina."

"Nakina? You found out where she's living?"

"Yeah."

"Where?"

"Downtown."

"That's good, but can't you go another time?"

"No, I already told her I was coming." I didn't normally lie to my parents but it seemed easier than explaining. Still, it would have been nice to go with them. Mom had been in a good mood lately and we were having fun together doing Christmas baking like the old days.

I helped Mom wrap up the Noel Log—a thin chocolate cake rolled up with mocha cream inside, then covered with chocolate icing. I always made the bark pattern with a fork. It looked like real bark. Then we'd put a plastic holly berry thingy on top. Fort McKay tradition. Like George the Porter, who's this black railway porter guy who drives Santa's sleigh. Seriously. George the Porter. In Fort McKay Christmas was a weird mess of Jesus, Mary, Santa Claus and George the Porter all mixed up like a tub full of guts.

"So what's Nakina doing now?" Mom asked.

"Not sure."

"Is she going to finish her grade twelve?"

"Don't know."

"Here, put tinfoil over the cardboard."

I wrapped the tinfoil around the cardboard so Mom could put the Noel Log on it. The kitchen smelled like chocolate.

"Perfect." Mom put her arm around my waist and we admired our handiwork. Another perfect Noel Log.

As I watched our car pull out of the driveway I had a sudden urge to run after it. I wanted to be with them, sitting in the back seat of the warm car holding the Noel Log and listening to Dad singing Christmas carols off key. Didn't even know if I could find Nakina, so what was the point.

I got dressed and headed out. In the north you can always tell how cold it is by the sound of the snow when you walk. The lower the temperature the louder the crunch. That night it had a high squeaking crunch. Very cold. By the time I got to First Avenue my hands were getting numb. I was glad the canvas was small—it would have been a pain to haul a big honkin thing all that way. I turned onto Simpson Street and checked the address on the paper I'd stuffed into my coat pocket. It was still farther down.

Simpson Street was rough. No nice way to put it. Drunks, hookers and magazine stores that didn't sell *Ladies Home Journal*. I passed the Polish Legion, where Dad picked up perogies every Thursday night, and the Greyhound bus terminal, where an old guy was sitting propped up against the wall. I stepped over his legs thinking someone should haul the poor guy inside before he froze.

A little farther along I saw two women outside the Empire Hotel. They were standing at the edge of the sidewalk like they were waiting for a bus, but I figured it was more likely they were waiting for business. Cold night for hookers. A car pulled over and the driver leaned over to the passenger side and rolled down his window. One of the women stepped towards the car and leaned into the window, bending over so far her ass almost showed under her short coat. She chatted with the guy, then opened the door and got in. When the car drove away her friend stepped up to the curb rocking back and forth on high-heeled boots like she was trying to keep her legs warm. She turned her head and looked down the street for cars.

This is what I remember. Nakina was wearing a fur coat like the one she had tried on in Portland's that day. Her long black hair blew across her face and she flicked it back. She saw me.

I turned and ran. Fast. I could hear her shouting but I didn't turn around.

chapter nine

I don't remember much, even now. Funny how the brain works. Maybe it's a protective thing, like blocking bad shit out so it can't hurt you. I don't remember walking home, don't remember the cold and don't remember passing anyone in the street.

I remember lying on my bed with my coat still on, clutching the damn painting under my arm. I remember being glad Mom and Dad weren't back yet because I didn't want them to see me crying. I remember being angry, then I guess I fell asleep because I remember dreaming about the Stone Man. I stood on the wharf in front of Sask Pool 7 and tried to shout, "Help!" but no words came out. The Stone Man sat up, unfolded his arms and held them out to me. I slipped off the dock and walked across the surface of the water to him. The Stone Man, Nanna Bijou, wrapped his big stone arms around me and I could feel my own nana's arms around me. I could feel my face nestled soft in her big warm chest and she said, "It's OK honey. Everything is going to be OK."

Knocking at the front door woke me up. I went downstairs half asleep thinking Mom and Dad must have forgotten their key. I opened the door and it was two cops. Bernie Olfson was standing at my door. The other cop was talking to me but I didn't hear what he was saying because I was staring at Bernie Olfson standing at my door. Olfson took a step towards me, inside my house, in the middle of the night. He put his hand on my shoulder, and I screamed and screamed and screamed.

I remember shouting, "Don't touch me" and hitting him in the chest and face. The other cop grabbed my arms and I thought he was going to push me down onto the floor. I kept screaming and he let go of my arms, and then I saw a neighbour running across the street towards me.

After that there are just bits and pieces. A face, a few words. Anna's mom holding me. The house full of people. Casseroles. Piles of casseroles and squares in Pyrex dishes on the kitchen counter.

That's what my family did when someone died. Made squares. I used to call Nanaimo bars Dead Squares 'cause you'd always get them at a funeral. There were lots of Dead Squares in my kitchen and strange women and relatives I didn't know and strange cars in the driveway.

Nobody talked to me, which was good.

But they talked about me, which wasn't good.

Everyone was gathered in the kitchen so I went into the living room to get away. The tree was still up. The goddamn Christmas tree still standing there all glittery and pretty. There were presents under the tree. I knelt down and picked up the one I'd wrapped for Mom—a bracelet with her birthstone. I put it down beside Dad's present—a bunch of boating magazines. Behind the tree was a large box with my name on it. From Santa. I opened it, and inside was a Nikon camera, zoom lens and camera bag. A Nikon. I curled over the box sobbing, and after awhile I could feel someone behind me holding me.

The day of the funeral Anna's mom helped me get dressed. I forgot how to get dressed. Eighteen years old and I sat at the end of the bed holding my bra in my hands and I couldn't remember how to put it on. So Anna's mom sat beside me on the bed and handed me stuff.

The coffins at the front of the church were closed. Someone had put photos on top of them. One of my mom when she worked for the Red Cross during the war; she was wearing her uniform and she looked really tough and really beautiful. The photo on my dad's coffin was of him standing beside his racing boat. He was hoisting a trophy over his head and had a big silly grin on his face. With his curly hair he still looked like a kid.

There was another one of them together in a canoe. Dad was at the back paddling and Mom was leaning back on him, and her hair was falling over his legs. They looked young and happy.

I looked down at my feet and saw two black shoes and I wondered where they had come from and when I'd put them on. Maybe I didn't put them on. Maybe those weren't my feet.

People were praying and singing hymns but I felt like I was floating under water. The minister stood at the front with his mouth opening and shutting like a fish but I couldn't hear any words. People stood up and sat down but I sat staring straight ahead. Then eight men went to the front of the church. I recognized a couple of uncles and the rest were guys my dad worked with I think.

They stood around the two coffins and grabbed the brass bars along the sides, and when the organ began to play "Abide with Me" they carried the coffins down the middle aisle. The people around me started to cry, and that scared me. I didn't know what to do. Someone was making moaning sounds like an animal caught in a trap. I started to shake and realized the moaning sounds were coming from me. I couldn't stand up. Everyone was standing up but I just folded up and turned my head away so I couldn't see the coffins being carried out.

Someone put an arm around me. It was Anna. She said "Stand up Molly." I stood up. She put one arm around my waist and balanced herself on her cane. When I got out into the aisle behind the coffins I felt my legs wobble and another arm held me. Anna's mom on the other side. I let them carry me out of the church.

Outside snow was falling. It fell softly on the steeple of the church and on the two oak coffins being carried down the stairs. Snow fell silently on the roofs of the two black hearses and muted the sound of traffic in the street. As I walked down the steps I could feel snowflakes melting down the back of my neck.

That night after the funeral I put on my parka and took my blankets and pillows out to the garage. I crawled into Dad's boat and made a nest under the deck. I thought I would feel safe there but I didn't. I felt like a rogue wave was about to swamp the boat and take me down.

Oh yeah, here's another Fort McKay Christmas tradition—every Christmas Eve someone goes out partying and gets shit-faced drunk then gets in their car and wipes out some nice happy family. On Christmas Eve 1970, it was my nice happy family. My nice happy family, minus one. I was supposed to be in the car with them.

book two

chapter ten

was living with Anna then. My rich aunt and uncle had finally made some lame offer to take me in, but come on. I made an excuse about wanting to finish Grade 12 at my own school and they seemed happy to be off the hook. They high-tailed it back to North Fort and their martinis.

Anna's mom came and got me. Didn't say anything, just came over and took me home with her. And that was OK by me.

I called Anna's mom Kiiko and her dad Toivo and we all got on OK. I learned to eat *puuro* for breakfast and *pulla* bread and *lihapullat,* which is just meatballs. We played cards, and some nights Anna and I drank beer at the Wayland with her dad and his buddies from the mill.

About a month after the accident Kiiko and I walked back to my house carrying empty cardboard boxes. The house had to be sold. I knew that. A bunch of ladies from the neighbourhood came over with sandwiches, and Toivo and a friend parked their trucks outside ready to haul stuff away. Kiiko got everyone organized, and sent the ladies into the living room and basement. She took me up to my parent's bedroom and I sat on the bed as she went through their things.

"Molly."

I looked up at Kiiko. "Sorry, what did you say?" I wasn't listening. I was thinking how weird it was to be sitting on Mom and Dad's bed while Kiiko went through their closets.

"I've got your mom's jewelry box."

"OK."

"I'll put it in here honey, and anything you want to keep just put in the box at the end of the bed."

"It's OK. I don't need anything."

Kiiko put down the armful of clothes she was holding and sat beside me. I picked up the fur coat from the top of the pile. My grandmother's beaver coat. I ran my hand across the short soft fur.

"You want me to do this?" she asked. "If it's too hard I can do it."

"I just can't…"

"It's OK, I'll finish this. You go on home."

Home. That was the problem. I was home. I went out of my house with my grandmother's fur coat over my arm and walked down the sidewalk. Before I turned onto Anna's street I looked back to see some men carrying our sofa down the front stairs and putting it in the back of the truck.

I finished high school. My marks were crap but they cut me some slack, I guess because of the dead parents thing, and said as long as I showed up for classes I'd graduate.

I got up, had breakfast, brushed my teeth, went to school. All the normal stuff. Normal from the outside.

Inside I felt like I'd gone insane. I remember once when I was about eight I got invited to a pajama party at Linda Dell's house. It was a big deal because I'd never been to a sleepover before, and well, to be honest, I wasn't usually invited to parties. It was fun at first. We played games, ate pizza, and I showed them how I could make pop squirt out my nose. They liked that. Then it was time to crawl into the sleeping bags and that's when it hit me. I wanted to go home. I hated being in a strange house with someone else's parents. I wanted my dad to come in and kiss me on the forehead and say "Goodnight sweetie," like he did every night. I wanted Mrs. Dell to call my dad and tell him to come and get me. Right away.

That's how I felt the year after the accident. I felt like I was curled up inside my sleeping bag, crying so no one could hear me, so no one would know how scared I was, waiting for my dad to come and take me home.

───────◇───────

Everyone was careful not to talk about the accident. Nobody spoke about my mom and dad. I got it. It was best to pretend that nothing had happened because it upset people.

Since I couldn't talk *about* my parents I talked *to* them. Every day, in my head I told them stuff I was doing, just normal stuff like what I was eating or what was happening at school and funny stuff the neighbours were doing that would have made them laugh.

Sometimes at night, in bed, when I was almost asleep I got angry. I was angry with them for leaving me. I knew the accident wasn't their fault, that they didn't want to die. I got that, but it didn't matter. What mattered was that they were gone and I was alone. What the hell was I supposed to do?

I guess I was pissed off with everything that year. With school and my teachers and the lawyer who kept asking me to come by his office to sign papers. I didn't want to sign papers. I didn't want to talk to some fucking lawyer about my parents being dead.

I was pissed off with Nakina too. She never came to the funeral. I needed her.

"Who the hell is St. Urho?" Anna had dragged me to a parade in front of the Finlandia Club.

"Patron saint of Finland. He chased the grasshoppers out of Finland."

"No shit."

"I want to get to the front; I can't see anything," she said.

"I hate parades."

"Philistine."

"Seriously. If there's clowns or bagpipes…"

"Bagpipes? Idiot, it's a Finnish parade!"

I moved to the front of the crowd in time to see an eight-foot grasshopper coming down the street. The giant bug was strung up between two poles. Four Finlanders were holding the ends of the poles on their shoulders and they were hauling that big-ass bug down the street.

"Told you."

"OK. So how did this St. Arsehole…"

"St. Urho."

"St. Urho guy drive the grasshoppers out of Finland?"

"Dunno."

"What were they doing there in the first place?"

"Shut up and watch the parade."

Behind the giant grasshopper was a mess of people carrying pitchforks and rakes, and behind that a half-ton truck hauling a polka band and everybody was screaming, "*Heinäsirkka, heinäsirkka, mene täältä hiiteen,*" which means something like "go to hell grasshopper." Funny stuff.

After the polka band rolled by everyone poured in behind and followed the parade into the Finlandia Club where the singing and dancing carried on all night.

"So when did this St. Urho guy drive the grasshoppers out of Finland?" I was sitting at a table in the Finlandia Club, with Anna and Toivo drinking green beer. Green for grasshoppers.

"He didn't."

"You told me he did."

"Ya, well I was just screwing with you."

"Fuck off. Seriously."

"Seriously. The whole thing was invented by some guy in Minnesota a few years ago."

I thought it was funny—the parade, the big freakin grasshopper. My dad would have split a gut laughing. And suddenly I wanted him with me, sitting beside me drinking green beer. Most of the time I was alright, but sometimes, when I wasn't expecting it, grief punched me hard in the gut. I guess I was looking pretty serious, because Anna knocked me on the shoulder and said, "Molly. Lighten up, it's a party!"

Grief did strange things. Before the accident I was addicted to reading, but afterwards words jumped around on the page and didn't mean anything. I couldn't figure out the code. After a while I gave up trying. Didn't want to read, didn't want to do anything. Not a fucking thing.

One day about three months after the accident I picked up a copy of *Slaughterhouse Five*. Had to. English assignment.

"Molly, you're next, could you come to the front please." Miss Sewell was my Grade 12 English teacher. She was good—really knew her stuff, and she tried to encourage me. I knew she was trying to help, but I was a lost cause.

I went up to her desk and stood looking out the window for a while. There were clouds in the sky that looked like big fat butts floating by.

"Molly, are you ready?"

"Yeah. OK. So, my book was *Slaughterhouse Five* by Kurt Vonnegut." I looked down at my notes and the letters were dancing all over the page. I shook my head to see if I could get the flippin letters to stand still. I heard someone at the back laughing.

"So, my book was *Slaughterhouse Five* by Kurt Vonnegut. Kurt Vonnegut Jr." I cleared my throat and looked at the words. They were still bouncing around and I couldn't catch my breath.

"So. It's about this guy Billy Pilgrim who goes off to war and comes home nuts." I headed back to my seat.

"Molly."

"Yeah."

"Could you come back up please."

"Yeah OK." I could hear some kids at the back of the room laughing their heads off.

"Could you tell us, in your own words, what the novel is about?"

I stood looking at my feet. Pretty small feet really. Which is weird because I'm so tall.

"Molly?"

I kept my head down so I wouldn't have to look at anyone. "So, Billy Pilgrim, when he was a kid, his dad threw him in the swimming pool to teach him how to swim but Billy sank to the bottom."

"Loser!" Jackie Slaunwaite shouted from the back of the room and everyone broke out laughing.

I looked at Jackie. "It wasn't that he *couldn't* swim. He just didn't want to. So he got sent off to war and he was a crap soldier. He didn't want to be there, but he ended up in Germany and got taken prisoner of war and was locked in a meat slaughterhouse. And that's where he was during the Dresden firebombing. So when it's over Billy comes out of the slaughterhouse and everything is flattened. Burnt to a crisp. And they make him dig the burned bodies out of the rubble. So Billy's digging up bodies and he gets unstuck in time. He's zapping back and forth from the present to the past and then suddenly, whap—he's in the future and gets kidnapped by these aliens who look like upside-down toilet plungers."

Jackie started laughing again. Probably the toilet plunger thing.

"Anyway Kurt Vonnegut was Billy. He was in Dresden during the firebombing. He was just trying to say that war is crap."

I walked toward my seat, crumpling my paper into a ball.

"Molly, could you stay at the front for a moment while…"

I ignored Miss Sewell and walked past my seat, out the door, down the hall and out of the school. I walked across the parking lot, along the river and didn't stop walking till I was deep in the bush.

Shit happens. People die. So it goes.

chapter eleven

At least *Slaughterhouse Five* got me reading and I started hanging out at the library again. Miss Black, the librarian, seemed glad to see me.

"Molly, do you have any plans for the summer?"

"No, not really." I'd known Miss Black since I was a little kid. She used to let me help shelve the books. Funny thing though, I never really knew anything about her. She was just Miss Black, short and round and nice. I think she liked her job, and she liked kids. I think she liked me. When I was little I used to think she lived in the library and I imagined that when they turned off the lights and locked the doors at night she'd still be sitting in her chair behind the reference desk.

So here's something about Miss Black. The day of the funeral, when I was walking out behind the coffins, I saw her sitting in the church. She didn't have to be there, wasn't like she was family or anything, but she came.

"The library got a LIP grant."

"A lip grant? A grant for lips?"

"L.I.P.—Local Initiative Project. One of Trudeau's ideas."

I noticed that Miss Black always blushed a little when she talked about Pierre. I think Pierre was her Leonard.

"The grant is to catalogue our photograph collection. Would you be interested?"

"Maybe. I don't know. I've never done anything like that before."

"It's simple. You just have to number the photographs and file them.

"OK. I guess so."

"Good. Come back tomorrow afternoon and Mr. Klein will interview you."

"Who?"

"Mr. Klein, the new chief librarian."

I went to the library the next day and Miss Black took me behind the check-out desk and down a hallway past framed black and white photos of old guys in suits. Former chief librarians. As we walked into Mr. Klein's office I was wondering why the chief dudes were all guys and the librarians were all women.

"Mr. Klein, this is Miss Bell. She's here to interview for the cataloguing project."

"Have a seat Miss Bell. I don't know how much Miss Black has told you about the project."

"Not much." I was thinking he looked younger than I expected—maybe late twenties.

"Well, the grant is for three months and basically the job is to catalogue the library's historical photograph collection."

"Yeah."

The hours are nine to five, Monday to Friday."

"OK."

"Are you interested?"

"Yeah."

"We're looking for someone to start right away."

"OK."

"OK, you can start right away?"

"Yeah." I knew I sounded like an idiot but I couldn't think of anything else to say. I wasn't really paying attention because I was looking at his dark eyes and his black curly hair, which was pretty long for a chief librarian if you asked me. He had a weird accent and was wearing these thick, black-frame glasses, and I could see his lips moving but I was thinking…Woody Allen. This guy reminds me of Woody Allen. So I just kept nodding and saying, "Yeah."

"Good, well you can start Monday then."

"Seriously?"

"Yes. Is that OK?

"Sure."

Monday morning at five to nine I was standing at the front door of the library. It was locked, of course, because the library didn't open until ten. So I was standing there with my knees shaking and my palms sweating thinking maybe I should have paid more attention when Mr. Klein was talking instead of thinking about how long his hair was.

"Miss Bell?"

It was Mr. Klein.

"It's locked." I said.

"I know, that's why I told you to use the back door. Follow me."

I followed him around the building to a small door near the back parking lot.

"You can leave your coat here in the lunchroom. We have coffee at ten and we have tea around three in the afternoon. You're welcome to join us."

I followed Mr. Klein into the basement, past the furnace room to a small room with cement walls and no windows.

"I'm sorry, it's not a great spot, but it's the only space we've got."

"It's fine." I said.

There was a small oak desk and chair, a grey metal filing cabinet and stacks of cardboard boxes piled up beside the cabinet. Mr. Klein opened one of the boxes.

"Go through each box; they're in no particular order. Each photo will need an accession number and you'll have to devise a numbering system. Once you've entered the number on the photo you can put the number on the index card along with a description of the photo. If the photo falls into several categories you can fill out additional index cards and cross-reference. Then, once you've finished with the photo you can put it into one of these acid-free envelopes."

Now that really struck me as funny. I mean, acid-free envelopes—envelopes that weren't on acid?

Mr. Klein continued. "Put the accession number on the envelope, then file each photo numerically in this filing cabinet."

"Right."

"Any questions?"

"No."

"Good. I'm just upstairs if you do have any questions."

I was glad when he left. I sat down at my desk. Liked the sound of that, my desk. My office. My job. I had a job. Ha, good on ya, Molly. But I was going to lose it fast if I didn't get my shit together so I took a handful of photos out of the box and placed them on the desk beside the index cards. Numbering system. The first thing I had to do was come up with a numbering system. Not hard, I liked systems. I'm very anal that way.

I came up with a system where every photo got a number, starting with the number one, then the year of the photograph, like 1907, then the subject, like grain elevators or people:

1. 1897—People—Wedding of Charles Tuppen and Vera Books.

2. 1908—Elevators—Fire at Elevator B.

3. 1951—Railway—Chief Andrew Bannon gives peace pipe to Donald Gordon, president of the C.P.R., Sept 27.

I had a stack of lined index cards and I wrote the number on the back of each photograph, then on the top corner of the index card. Then I wrote a description of the photo with as much information as I could find—names, buildings and addresses. I wrote an index card for the number, an index card for the year and an index card for the subject, and I cross-referenced each subject entry like crazy, sometimes doing a dozen cards for one photo. Like I said, I'm very anal.

6. 1911—Ship industry—S.S. Duluth pulling into dry dock at the Western Dry Dock and Ship Building Co. circa 1911. Beside the freighter is a dump scow under construction.

7. 1870—Banks—Teepee beside the site of the new Ontario Bank.

Teepee being pushed away for the bank, I thought. Two men with long braids are sitting on the ground outside the Teepee and a mean looking guy in a black suit and bowler hat is standing beside them. Find the banker.

8. 1919—People—Mrs. J.G. Podowosky.

Dead. Dead as a doornail, propped up in a chair dressed in her Sunday best. The photo was taken at J.R. Evans Photography Studio, so I thought the family must have thrown dead granny into the back of a truck and schlepped her off to Evan's photo studio. The family is all crowded in behind her with their best funeral faces on, and a man behind granny has his hand on her shoulder. Probably propping her up so she doesn't fall over while J. R. Evans snaps the photo. I guess the photo is to show the folks back home that granny was well and truly dead.

9. 1890—People—Prince Arthur, Duke of Connaught visits Fort McKay, May.

He is standing there with this long curly moustache and a pinched look on his face like he's constipated.

10. 1904—Communications—building the telegraph line from Heron Bay to Fort McKay. Left to right, George Peterson, Duncan McFee, Archibald Bell.

Archibald Bell, that's my great grandpa Archie. He was just a kid. Nice looking kid. I taped a photocopy of that photo above my desk. It was nice to look up and see my great grandpa smiling down on me.

> 11.1896—People—An unidentified man with four
> kids, all bundled in fur coats and fur hats, sitting on
> a sled pulled by two Newfoundland dogs.

Men going off to war. Men coming back from war. Men going off to another war. There was a photo of soldiers coming back from World War Two, getting off the train in South Fort. Between the train and the station was a long table filled with fancy rolled sandwiches with the crusts cut off and pots of tea and china teacups. On the back of the photo it said, "South Fort I.O.D.E. welcome men back from the front." I.O.D.E—Imperial Order Daughters of the Empire—there's a mouthful. I figured those poor soldiers were probably more interested in getting their hands on a cold beer and a hot girl than a rolled cucumber sandwich.

Photos of men in lacrosse uniforms standing in a long line on a frozen lake. The guy at the end, the captain of the team, was my great grandpa Archie's brother Joe. He died in the flu epidemic of 1918.

Photos of miners at Silver Mountain in 1883, and loggers in the bush north of Papoonge, and the three long buildings of the Gowanlock brickyards. Photos of men digging ditches along the first roads. First Avenue 1919 with wooden boardwalks. First Avenue 1953 with brick storefronts.

If you looked hard enough you could see stuff. You could see how the Ojibwe lived beside the Stone Man for hundreds of years, hunting and fishing and living off the land, then everything flipped ass-over-tits when the Europeans arrived. Guys in kilts and French voyageurs in canoes chasing beaver. Well, not chasing beaver exactly, though I'm sure they did a lot of that, but trapping beavers for pelts to make hats for the rich dudes back in Britain. This whole country got turned ass-over-tits because of beavers and hats. That's Canada for you.

I found a hand-drawn map labelled "1878"—around the time my great grandpa emigrated from Colonsay, Scotland. There were about twelve houses in a circle near the waterfront. My great grandpa helped to put up the first telegraph lines and his parents ran the telegraph office from their attic. Then came the railway and things went ass-over-tits again. The rails hooked the town up to the outside world. People came from all over—Sweden, Finland, Italy, the Ukraine. Buildings boomed, elevators boomed, jobs boomed. One minute there's nothing here but bush, then overnight it's the flippin Chicago of the North. Or at least that's what those rich Brits who ran the town thought. And I guess for a while it was. At least for them.

I got the hang of the cataloguing, and soon I couldn't wait to get to the library in the morning to see what I was going to find in my pile of photographs. Mr. Kline invited me up to the lunchroom for my breaks, but I wasn't interested in sitting around with a bunch of people I didn't know, trying to make nice. After a while he started coming downstairs in the afternoon with two mugs of tea. We got talking, and I realized he wasn't as stiff as he seemed when I first met him. It was pretty clear from his accent he wasn't from Fort McKay, so one day I finally asked him where he was from.

"New York," he said.

"So what are you doing here?"

"Draft dodger."

"You actually got drafted?"

"I did. Got my notice, packed a bag and flew to Canada that day."

"OK, I get coming to Canada, but why Fort McKay?"

"I went to Montreal first and studied at McGill for a couple years. Then this job came up and here I am."

"Can you ever go back?"

"I don't know. There might be an amnesty for draft dodgers once the war is over. Hard to say."

"Must have been tough to leave your country not knowing if you can ever go back," I said.

"I didn't have a choice. It was either come to Canada or fight in a war I didn't believe in."

I remembered all the years of watching the Vietnam War on television—people getting blown up and burned up, and I knew that if I was a young guy living in the States I'd get my ass up to Canada too.

———✧———

I started looking forward to my three o'clock visit from Mr. Klein. We'd drink tea and talk and as I listened to him talk about his life back in the States I realized we had something in common. We'd both been separated from our families, and we were both stuck in the bush in the middle of nowhere.

"Hey, look at this." I passed Mr. Klein a photo I had found.

"What is it?"

"It's the Mariaggi Hotel in 1884, the year it was built. Says here it was considered one of the grandest hotels in Canada at the time."

"Is it still standing?"

"Yeah, but it sure doesn't look like this. It's a dump. I think Social Services owns it now. A lot of homeless people live there." I read from a newspaper clipping taped to the back of the photo: "The dining room was hung with Union Jacks from one end of the hall to the other and two long tables ran the length of the room. Around the tables was a miniature railway track with trains and a telegraph line making up the story of the completion of the track."

"So what was the dinner for?" he asked.

"Something to do with the building of the railway I guess. Look, they even give the menu: Lake Superior whitefish, braised fillet of beef, roast partridge with bacon and for dessert Charlotte Russe—whatever that is."

Mr. Klien picked up another clipping: "Three hundred guests gathered for the grand march descending the staircase into the ballroom for the Bal Poudre."

"What's a Bal Poudre?" I asked.

"It means literally 'powdered wig ball.'"

Mr. Klein passed the clipping to me and I saw the ladies in their fancy ball gowns coming down a winding staircase. "Hard to believe this town was such a happening place back then," I said.

That afternoon I spent hours cataloguing each of the Mariaggi photographs and cross-referencing them by the names of the people, the clothing and the events. I made a photocopy of the Bal Poudre and put it over my desk, beside the photo of my great grandfather.

After work I walked out of the library along First Avenue. After a long day in the basement looking at old photos it was hard to get my head back into the present. I felt like Billy Pilgrim—unstuck in time. One minute I'm walking down First Avenue in 1971, then zap, it's 1898 and there's a dirt road lined with wooden shacks, then zap, it's 1910 and there's a horse and carriage going by, then zap, it's 1958 and the Santa Claus parade is coming down a paved street.

I stopped on the street that evening and looked up at the clock on the tower of the Empire Building. It had stopped. I wondered when. I looked down the street again and I saw that everything had stopped. The front of the Odeon Theatre boarded up, Portland's Ladies Wear closed. There was a homeless shelter beside the Lorna Doone. The street was dead.

When did it happen? I looked down First Avenue again and felt like I was living in a ghost town. No rotten egg stink was coming out of the mill—the mill was shut down. No Auto Works rolling subway cars off the assembly line—the factory was closed. No grain being loaded into grain boats—the grain elevators had been empty since the grain started moving west to Asia.

I heard a plane overhead and looked up. Flying east. Probably filled with people with one-way tickets to Toronto. Lucky them.

chapter twelve

ate in August I found a stack of six cardboard boxes piled outside my office door. I went to Mr. Klein's office to find out what they were. He was talking on the phone and motioned for me to wait until he finished.

"You found the boxes?" he said when he hung up the phone.

"I did. What's in them?"

"I don't know. They were brought in yesterday. The woman who brought them said she works in the office at St. Mary's residential school. They're tearing it down apparently."

"Tearing it down? I didn't know that."

"She said she'd been a student at the residential school when she was a kid. Anyway she'd been told to shred these papers, but she brought them here and asked if the library would take them."

"Do the Sisters know she brought them here?"

"No, and she asked me not to tell anyone."

"So…"

"I'll have a look through first, make an inventory of what's there. If there are important papers I think I may have to hand them over to the Sisters of St. Mary's."

"I could do that for you."

"What's that?"

"Have a look through the boxes. Make an inventory."

"I couldn't pay you, Molly."

"That's OK. I could do it on my lunch break. Do a bit each day."

"That would be great, if you're sure you don't mind. It's a lot of work."

"I'd like to do it." I hesitated. "I had a friend who was there."

"At the residential school? What was it like?"

"I don't really know. Bad I think. She didn't talk about it much. I think stuff happened there. Stuff people didn't talk about. I think the church tried to cover things up."

Each day at noon I ate my lunch at my desk and unpacked the boxes from the residential school. In a lined journal Mr. Klein had given me I listed everything I found. In the boxes I found journals from the 1940s with the names of students and their places of birth. I found files with correspondence between the Department of Indian Affairs and the Catholic Diocese. Looked like important stuff. I found photos of students standing in front of the school and photos of inside the classrooms. I found newspaper clippings from the local paper. I found letters from parents.

One afternoon Mr. Klein came downstairs with two mugs of tea and I showed him some of the documents I'd found.

He looked at two letters—one from a parent saying her

child had been beaten, and the response from the school administrator denying any mistreatment.

"So there's more correspondence there?" Mr. Klein said. "More letters like these?"

"Lots more. And one whole box is filled with lists of all the students. Some of the stuff looks really old. You're not going to give these papers back to the church, are you?"

Mr. Klein was quiet for a moment while he read through one of the documents I'd given him. When he looked up he said, "Lets finish the inventory first. Once that's done I'll decide what to do with them."

Over the next few weeks I continued going through the boxes, and the more I went through the correspondence the more I understood why the church wanted to destroy the records. I started making photocopies of some of the documents for myself. I didn't tell Mr. Klein, just slipped them in with the papers I was photocopying for the cataloguing project. I took them home to read through when I had more time.

One Saturday I took my camera and walked to the residential school. I arrived as the sun was rising. I wanted to catch the changing light. I stood behind the chain-link fence and took photos of the demolition crane in front of a pile of rubble and bricks. I could see the back wall and the narrow interior walls on each floor. The back section of the roof was intact but the front of the roof was gone. It was like looking into a giant dollhouse.

I took my camera bag off of my shoulder and screwed

on my close-up lens. I took shots through the fence of the exposed belly of the school. The sun was just above the horizon and there was a subtle change in light, silhouetting the dark walls of the building against the soft blue-gray of the morning sky behind.

I walked the length of the fence and found an opening I could squeeze through. Once inside I checked to see if anyone had seen me. There was no one around. I walked through the piles of bricks, shooting everything I saw. I knelt down and took a photo of the shards of stained glass from the chapel window. I noticed something under the glass and reached down carefully to pick up a small black shoe. The shoe of a child, maybe five years old. I held the shoe in my hand, so small and worn, and wondered where the child was now. I thought about Nakina and wondered how old she was when she was brought here?

When I stood up I saw bright fingers of light coming through the cracks in the crumbling wall. I took that shot, light breaking through darkness. I tucked the tiny shoe in my pocket and made my way back to the other side of the fence.

Before I left I turned to take one last shot. I stood on the spot where I had first seen Nakina, fingers curled over the top of the chain-link fence. I raised my camera and looked through the lens: crumbling walls of brick and broken glass. All the children gone. Nakina gone.

My job at the library ended in September. On my last day Mr. Klein took me out for coffee to the greasy spoon across from the library.

"You did a great job with the photos, Molly," he said.

"Thanks."

"Have you ever thought of going to library school?"

"No. Not really."

"If you ever do, I'd be happy to give you a reference. You have a very organized mind and good attention to detail."

"I always thought I was just anal and boring."

"Two essential qualities for a librarian."

"I'll keep that in mind."

"I haven't told anyone yet, but I applied for a job in Montreal," he said.

"So you're leaving?"

"Just heard back today. They've offered me the job."

"Congratulations."

"Molly, you know those papers from the residential school?"

"Yeah."

"I've put them in the archives, in the basement behind the closed stacks. They are in a box labeled SMP."

"SMP?"

"St. Mary's Papers."

"I'm glad you kept them," I said.

When we got back to the library Mr. Klein gave me a gift, a mug with the library crest on it.

"Thanks," I said. "It will remind me of our afternoon tea breaks together. I really enjoyed them." I put on my coat. "Good luck in Montreal."

"Thank you."

As I left the library I was surprised how sad I felt to be saying goodbye.

———◆———

That night Anna took me downtown for drinks to celebrate. "So, what are you going to do, Molly?" she asked.

"Order a rye and ginger."

"Ha funny. And after that?"

"What?" I was trying to stuff Anna's canes under the chair across from us.

"Seriously. What's your plan?" she asked.

"No plan."

"I thought you were going to art school," she said.

"Stupid idea."

"No it's not. You've got talent."

"I'm crap."

"You give up too fast."

"Shut up."

"Why don't you apply at Lakehead? You could get in for the winter term."

"Don't want to go to Lunkhead."

"Confederation College?

"What for?"

"I don't know. To get a job."

The band was playing "Stairway to Heaven" and a young guy came towards me looking like he was going to ask me to dance. I gave him my "fuck off" look and he backed right off. Nice to have power.

Anna changed the subject. "Hey, do you ever see Nakina?"

"No."

"Too bad," she said.

"No loss. Hey, lets get out of this place. It's dead in here."

We went back to the Wayland Hotel after and had a blast with all the ole guys buying us drinks. The band from the Legion was playing a Johnny Cash tune and Anna and I went up on stage, grabbed the mike and started singing. Don't know if we were any good or if everyone was just so completely shit-faced that it sounded good, but man, the crowd loved us that night.

Anna went to the ladies room, or the "ladies and escorts" room as it's known at the Wayland. She came out weaving and wobbling her way across the floor and I noticed something creeping below the hem of her skirt—her underwear was heading south. She couldn't let go of her canes to grab them so before she knew it she was flying the flag at half-mast. I suppose I should have given her a hand but it was so damned funny. She started laughing so hard I thought she'd have a stroke. I eventually got up and helped her back to the ladies and escorts room but we were both so drunk I don't know who was escorting who.

We closed down the Wayland that night and Toivo carried Anna home. Good times.

I was sitting in Anna's room one night. We were listening to John Lennon. Loved John. When the Beatles split up I went with John. We were lying on our beds drinking a bottle of Old Sailor, smoking Cameos and listening to "Imagine."

"I'm thinking of moving out," I said.

"What?"

"I'm going to get a place of my own."

"Why."

"Don't want to be a nuisance."

"You're not. You're a pain in the ass, but not a nuisance."

"Thanks."

"Where would you go?"

"In the bush."

"The bush. Seriously. You're moving into the bush?"

"Maybe."

"Why? You've been bitching for years about wanting to get out of this town, and now you've got the chance to get out and you're going into the bush?

"Yeah."

"Don't be an idiot, Molly. Get out. Travel. Go to art college. You've got the money."

Anna was right about the cash. I had this uncle who sold life insurance. Uncle Tommy used to come by the house about once a month with a bottle of rye and plunk himself down in the kitchen. He'd sit there getting shit-faced and the only way Dad could get rid of him was to buy insurance. So Dad bought life insurance. A lot of life insurance. Lucky me.

Anna was right about art school too. As long as I could remember I'd been planning my big escape from Fort McKay. I was going to go to art college—had it picked out. The Nova Scotia College of Art and Design.

What I couldn't explain to Anna was that after the accident everything changed. I changed. I'd tried a few times to fill out the application form for NSCAD but I couldn't do it. It wasn't that I didn't want to go. I just didn't think I was good enough. I figured that if I didn't apply I couldn't be rejected. Simple.

Next day I told Anna's dad I was moving out and wanted

to get a place as far back in the bush as I could get. Toivo took me to the Wayland and introduced me to a buddy from the mill who had a place for sale in Kamanistiquia.

Forbes Township, Kamanistiquia. Now that's out there. Fifty miles out of town, off the highway, down a dirt road just wide enough to get a car down. The nearest house was more than five miles away.

I bought a car from an old lady across the street. Sixty-nine white Dodge Polara with red leatherette seats. Leatherette sounded so much classier than plastic. And it had a slant six engine. Don't know why it mattered that the engine was on a slant, but it sounded hot.

I loaded it up with all my worldly belongings. I packed a garbage bag with my clothes and my grandmother's old fur coat. I packed up all my canvases and easel and my acrylic paints and brushes. I packed some pots and pans that Kiiko gave me and three shoeboxes full of photos. I filled the trunk with canned food, a huge box of tea, a bushel of apples, a ten-pound bag of rice and three big plastic containers of drinking water. I didn't know how safe the well water was. Bought an axe and a box of tools. I also packed the box of photocopies of the papers from the residential school. Toivo gave me a couple of bottles of wine and a case of beer. Kiiko was baking like crazy, and the last thing I loaded into the car was a large bag of homemade bread and my favourite sour cream coffee cake.

I knew Toivo and Kiiko weren't happy about me moving out to the bush—no power, no phone, no one around for miles. But it suited me just fine. I wanted to be alone.

chapter thirteen

moved out in the fall and worked like a bugger to get the place ready for winter. There were trees to cut, wood to split and food to store. Looked like there was about three cords of wood already cut, but I needed to cut another cord that would be seasoned and ready to burn by spring. I was glad dad taught me how to handle an axe. It was quiet. Blue jays woke me up in the morning with their shrieking, and sometimes I could hear squirrels snipping at each other, but most of the time it was completely silent.

The day after I got there I pushed an old wooden wheelbarrow out into the field and turned it to face the sun. It didn't have sides, just a tipped up front so I could lie on it like a lounge chair. I stripped off my clothes—hey, who was going to see my skinny little body out there—and lay naked in the middle of the field. I could see the house at the front of the property and across the field the old barn. Farther out in the field I could see the sauna. Not another human for miles—just what I wanted.

I worked hard. Got water for washing from the well in the morning, stoked the woodstove, split wood, dried fruit. I peeled and cored the bushel of apples Kikko gave me, strung them through a rope and hung them above the woodstove to dry. I cut up old clothes I found in the place and chinked the holes in the logs. I chinked like mad because I knew the cold winter air would come through every bit of sunlight I could see through the logs.

The house had three rooms: kitchen, living room and bedroom. There was a narrow porch at the front. I nailed up planks of barn board for insulation in the living room and it looked good. I nailed hooks on the boards and hung some of my paintings. I set my easel up in the kitchen near the window and spread my paints on the faded oilcloth that covered the table.

At night, before I went to bed, I'd head out to the shitter. The outhouse was dark and full of bugs, and before long I figured it was easier to just go out in the field and squat under the stars. The sky was amazing—the Milky Way, the Little Dipper, Orion.

I walked the property. The deed said 186 acres, but I never walked it all. There was a logging road along one side that went up the hill and back about two miles. The woodlot was mostly spruce and pine with a bit of birch. My feet sank into a spongy blanket of needles as I walked. Farther back there were stands of black oak and aspen. Across the west field there was a path through the bush that led down to the Kamanistiquia River. The property line ran about a quarter mile along the river.

The house had been built by Kaapo and Lina Rintala. Finlanders. Socialists. Kaapo and Lina lived on the north side of the Kamanistiquia River with all the red Finns, and the more conservative white Finns lived on the south side. They built the house, did some farming, had some kids, and when the kids grew up they moved into town. That was in the 1930s. They never came back. Most didn't.

As winter set in my body clock began to change. I slept in late. When I got up I went outside to pee, came back in, stoked the stove and made a pot of tea. In the afternoon after splitting wood I slept. At night, after going out to pee, I would bring the lantern into the kitchen, stoke the stove and paint. Not the best light, but I was awake and felt like working. I slept, stoked the fire, painted, slept. Sometimes I ate, but I wasn't very hungry. Good thing. I didn't have much food.

I was re-working the painting of the clock on the Empire Building. Corrected the perspective and angles of the windows. It was in black and white like all the rest, and I had painted the hands of the clock red so you could see it was 4:35 in the afternoon.

Once the snow came I really got off the time grid. No clock, no calendar. No time. Didn't matter. No mirror either, which was good because I stopped washing when it got so cold that the water in the washbasin froze. I kept adding layers of clothes and didn't take them off to sleep because the fire in the stove burned down by morning and it was friggin cold. I wore a fur hat with flaps—a true northern girl—and I looked like a freak. There was a thermometer mounted outside the kitchen window. It got down as far as forty-eight below. I think it froze there. I kept adding layers and layers of clothes, and on top I wore my grandmother's beaver skin coat. The coat had been made by plucking out the long hairs of the beaver pelt and leaving the soft downy underfur. It really kept the cold out.

I knew I had to strip down eventually and wash, but that was hard to do in the bush in the winter. I'd be bursting to pee but put off going outside because it was too damn cold. I kept a piss pot inside and it froze, which was good because it didn't stink. But every few days I had to go out and dump the peesicle.

My brain froze. Couldn't hold a thought. Frozen brain on my skinny little stick body—brainsicle.

Funny things happen when you don't talk. I thought I'd talk out loud to myself but I didn't. I even stopped talking inside my head. Got into a weird zen place. I just *was*. Like the snow on the ground and the wolves in the hills and the logs in the walls. I just was. I sat in the kitchen in the cabin in the woods in the world. Didn't seem like it needed to be more complicated than that.

Anna drove out in December and freaked me out. I panicked when I saw the car coming down the road and I hid. She got out and tried to walk through the snow with her canes and went face first into the snow. When she started swearing I realized who it was—no one can cuss in Finnish like Anna.

We sat down at the kitchen table, and she was talking so loud it felt like she was screaming at me. At first I just sat watching her—forgot that two-way thing with talking. I forgot I was supposed to jump in and do my bit.

"You look like Mary Christmas," she said.

"Tis the season."

"Seriously. You look like a street person. When was the last time you had a bath and washed your hair?"

"When did I move out here?" I said.

"Thought so. Are you eating?"

"I'm hibernating."

"Mother's worried about you. I'm worried about you. Come back into town with me. Stay at our place, just for the winter. You'll freeze your ass off out here."

I laughed. I thought about getting so cold that body parts started dropping off and before you know it, plunk, there goes my ass. "No thanks. I'm good." I sat for a while, then realized it was my turn to say something. "How's school?"

"Hard. They throw everything at you in the first term to weed out the losers."

"How'd you do?"

"I passed."

"Well good on ya Finlander, you're not a loser."

"Thanks. I think you're getting bush wacky."

"Yeah, maybe. Is that your car?" I asked, trying to change the subject.

"Yeah…like it?"

"It's OK. Does it have hand controls?"

"Yeah."

"Was it hard to learn how to use them?" I asked.

"I don't know. I never learned any other way. Do you ever get freaked out here alone?"

"Just once. Heard a snowmobile up in the hills. Probably some redneck hunters."

"What did you do?"

"Blew out the lantern, put my head between my legs and kissed my ass goodbye."

"Ha. What about animals?"

"Mice and shrews. Lots of them. Excellent in stew."

"Gross."

"There's wolves up in the hills."

"Wolves?"

"Yeah. I see them at night when I go out to pee. They don't bother me, I don't bother them."

Anna looked at the paint tubes and brushes on the table. "You're painting."

"A bit."

She adjusted the metal grips of her canes around her forearms, got up and stood in front of the painting of the Empire clock on the easel. "Good stuff. Really."

"I've got a lot to learn. Perspective is all shit."

"So, learn. Go to art college."

"Yeah, yeah. We've had this conversation."

"Jeez, Molly, you can't just stay out here wasting…"

"Don't. OK?"

"You haven't shovelled out the car. Is it running?" she asked.

"Probably not. Can't plug it in out here. I haven't tried to start it since the mercury went below forty."

"Come back to town with me."

"No."

"You're nuts."

"I hate your face pretty much."

Anna left me groceries and Finnish coffee bread from the Kivela bakery. My favorite bread—I think it had cardamom or something in it. I was grateful for the food but I was glad to see the taillights of her car disappear down the road. I didn't want to see anyone. Not even Anna.

Couldn't tell Anna the real reason I wouldn't go back into town with her. Out here I didn't know what day it was, so I didn't know when it was Christmas Eve, so I didn't have to face the anniversary of the accident.

I never talked about my mom and dad but they were always inside my head. I tried to hang on to their voices and their faces and the way it felt when my mom ran her hands through my hair when she was talking to me. It was getting harder.

⸻

I liked seeing the wolves at night. Maybe they liked taking a frog at me too. Why not—something new to look at. At first they stayed up at the edge of the clearing having a howl fest. Then they came a bit closer. One night they circled the barn and stood about five feet from me. Grey wolf, *canis lupus*. I counted eight of them. The male at the lead stood about three feet high with a thick grey coat—pale cream under his belly, then a darker fringe of greyish-black along his back. There were two V's of black under his neck, and his slanted yellow eyes never left my face. I stood still and waited.

He moved slowly forward, bringing the other seven with him. I could see a smaller wolf at his side, and behind him two pups that had probably been born that summer. The others, as tall as the lead wolf, held back a bit. They crouched with heads lowered. Submission. A few steps closer and I could see the black line of his mouth, smirking.

A few feet closer now. About two feet away. I wanted to touch him. I wanted to feel the coarse fur at the side of his face. I wanted to run my hands over the short sharp ears. His legs were long and powerful. I tried not to breathe.

He dipped his head, then looked at me again, and when he turned his head to the side the whole pack turned and walked back into the night. They stopped and turned one more time, frozen, staring at me, then trotted off into the bush.

A few minutes later I heard a howl—one long sad note. Silence, then the echo howled back across the valley. Silence again.

It was January or February, I don't know. It kept getting bloody colder. The thermometer stayed at minus forty-eight so I knew it was stuck there. As I got colder, I got slower, and it got harder to get out from under the covers to stoke the stove or bring in wood. I got confused. I forgot to eat and sometimes when I woke up it was dark and I didn't know if I was supposed to be waking up or going to sleep. My dreams felt real. Reality was fuzzy.

One night I dreamt I was walking home on Christmas Eve. I was walking along Simpson street when my parent's car came around the corner. I looked up and saw my mom waving at me, and then in slow motion I watched a car come towards them, swerve and hit them head on. I woke up screaming.

After that I didn't want to go back to sleep, so I slipped on my boots, grabbed the fur coat beside the bed and went into the kitchen. It was dark. I checked the woodstove and saw the fire was almost out. The embers were flickering red and yellow under the grey ash. I went to the wood box and took out the last two pieces. The fire caught but I needed more wood. I couldn't let the fire go down like that again. I pulled back the latch of the storm door and stepped outside.

As I inhaled frost formed on the inside hairs of my nose.

It hurt, so I opened my mouth to breathe and the cold cut my throat. I walked away from the house towards the wood-pile and as I walked the sky got brighter.

I looked up at the stars and felt a crazy burst of happy. The moon was almost full and sent a streak of light across the north hill. A path. I wanted to walk to the top of the hill on that path of light. I had it in my head that I could just walk up to the stars, so I stepped off the hard-packed snow and onto the icy top surface. It held. I moved forward and heard a crack but I didn't fall through. I was dancing on the snow, doing the northern girl rag. Rag momma rag, I was dancing my skinny little body up to the stars.

Shadows across the path. I stopped. He was back, with his yellow eyes on me. I could see the outlines of the others behind him. He smiled his dog-having-a-laugh smile. We stood still, together under the moon. I was one of the pack. I smelled their strong musky smell. I crouched down to be level with his eyes. I moved forward. I put my hands down so I was on all fours, almost touching his black nose. We were eye-to-eye and I could feel his hot sour breath. I waited for a sign. Waited for him to move forward.

Crack! The surface of the snow gave way and I fell through. He lunged back, baring his teeth—a deep growl vibrating in his throat. My arms and legs were stuck under me; I couldn't move. He stood over me, legs astride, shoulders raised. A fringe of hair rose around his face, two bared fangs inches above my forehead. The growl deepened.

I lowered my head. Submission.

He stepped back, turned his head. The pack turned and they were gone.

I watched them move into the shadows and I wanted to

follow. Pain ripped through my hip and snapped me out of my daydream and I thought, "Christ, what the hell am I doing here? What am I doing outside?"

I turned and saw the faint glow of light from the wood-stove through the kitchen window. Wasn't I just in there? Wasn't I just in the kitchen?

I tried to pull my arms out but my leg got wedged deeper in the snow. I was lying half in and half on the snow. I decided to rest, so I let my head fall back on the snow. I looked up at the sky. Beautiful. The stars were hanging there, so goddamned bright. And I was thinking, look at the stars just hanging there. Just hanging there. I thought I could hear the snow. I could feel the earth underneath the snow. I was lying on ground that had been there for billions of years—the Precambrian shield. I was lying there thinking all of this, and thinking nothing, just being in the universe under the stars.

Maybe I slept, I don't know. But when I opened my eyes the sky had changed. A line of blue dipped and swung up, then went yellow and red, then spread with jagged edges in waves across the North Mountain. Like a silk scarf snapping up and over, purple, red, then back to blue. I closed my eyes and heard the music. Aurora, Aurora Borealis. So beautiful. Warm, sleepy. I just wanted to go to sleep. Nice warm sleep.

And I'm lying on the back seat of the car coming back from Loon Lake. Curled up, warm, listening to my parent's voices. After awhile I hear Mom calling, "Wake up Molly we're home. Molly…Molly."

I don't want to wake up. I love sleeping in the back seat of the car feeling the road rock me like a cradle and hearing their voices droning away like a lullaby. I curl up more tightly and keep my eyes closed. I'm safe. Dad is driving; he's at the wheel. Everything is OK.

"Wake up, honey." It's Dad's voice this time. "Don't go to sleep now. Not now."

I opened my eyes, confused, and looked back at the house. I saw the light from the kitchen and remembered. I shouldn't have been outside. *Don't go to sleep. Get back inside. Fast.*

I couldn't feel my legs but crawled forward on my belly to the hard packed surface of the path. With my feet under me I tried to walk and oh god the pain. Tears fell and froze on my cheek. I got to the door and hit the handle with my arm because my fingers were numb. I got inside. The fire was almost out. Had to get more wood. I stumbled to the wood box and saw it was empty and I remembered why I was outside. To get wood. I went outside to get more wood.

I used my shoulder to knock open the door and went straight to the woodpile. I couldn't move my fingers, but rolled the logs up onto my arms and headed back inside. I dumped a large piece onto the fire and blew into the stove to bring the embers back to life. The log caught and I added three more. I went into the bedroom and using my closed fists pulled the blankets from my bed into the kitchen. I wrapped myself tight and lay on the floor beside the fire. As my body warmed, my fingers began to burn. I pulled back the blankets and looked at them. They were swollen and white. Madame Tussaud wax fingers.

Not good. Not good at all. I crossed my arms and tucked my white wax fingers into my armpits. The fire was going strong and I could feel the heat on my face. The armpit heat worked, but thawing the wax fingers brought more pain. I moaned and rocked and wept myself to sleep.

I dreamt about waking the Stone Man. I dreamt I was standing on the wharf and I shouted out to him and he sat up and smiled and waved at me, and as he waved, his stubby white stone fingers cracked and fell off.

When I looked at my hands next morning I saw how much I'd messed up. My fingers had turned purple and were swollen up like little sausages. Black blisters had formed on the fingertips and were oozing yellow pus.

After a few days my hands began to heal and the blisters closed over with a white crust. I had screwed up. I could see that. I fell asleep in the snow.

Here's the thing. When you're a northern girl there's one thing you know from the time you're born—you don't friggin fall asleep in the snow. If you do, you don't wake up.

chapter fourteen

Over the next few days I thought about what I had
done. I imagined Anna coming out in the spring
looking for me and finding my sorry old bones
out in the field. Not nice. Not nice for Anna. But I started
to think it wouldn't be nice for me either.

That's when it hit me that for a long time, ever since
the accident, I hadn't cared much about living. Not that
I'd actually thought about snuffing it—I was too chicken
for that. I couldn't stop thinking though that there'd been
a mistake the night of the accident. I was supposed to be
in the car with my mom and dad. I was supposed to be
dead.

I remembered a Dorothy Parker poem, "guns aren't law-
ful; nooses give; gas smells awful; you might as well live."
Well, after the night I almost died in the snow I decided,
what the hell, I might as well live.

I got my shit together. I kept the stove stoked and ate
three times a day. And I started to paint again. I put the

painting of Nakina in the Lorna Doone on the easel. It was like bringing Nakina into the cabin with me. I had thought I was happy with this painting, but looking at it again it looked so flat and naïve. I could see where I had gone wrong. It felt good to be able to see what wasn't working and try to find a way to take the image where I wanted it. So much I had to learn.

I was going through my stuff to find more paints when I came across the box with the papers from the residential school. I put it beside the kitchen table. I took an armful of papers out of the box and set them down on the table, and after getting a mug of tea from the pot on the woodstove I started to read.

April 3, 1921
To the Secretary of the Department of Indian Affairs from J.M. Bennett, School Inspector Lake Superior School district.

I respectfully ask the Department to do what they can to increase Indian attendance at the Fort McKay School. Built to accommodate a minimum of 50, yet they have never been sent more than 25. There is a large territory for the school to draw from, Heron Bay, Long Lake, Pic River, Pays Plat, the whole north shore of Lake Superior. The school is well adapted as a boarding school. Many Indian children coming to the school come knowing virtually no English and have no Christian belief. Care should be taken to see that they are of school age and in good health. It is required that an application be signed by one or both parents, along with

*a certificate of health. Catholic missionaries can assist
you in obtaining new pupils.*

The next letter came from Ottawa on May 4, 1923, from
the Department of Indian Affairs:

*We hope to substantially increase the numbers of
Indian children. In the meantime you can collect the
Indians needed from communities along the railway
lines.*

I read the last line again: You can collect the Indians
needed from communities along the railway lines. I remembered what Nakina had told me about the train that took
her away from her family and brought her to the residential
school in Fort McKay. Children collected like cargo from
along the railway lines to fill their quota.

The next letter was from Mary Wabashon of Pays Plat
to J.M. Bennett, School Inspector. Her son had been taken
from her and sent to the residential school. The next year the
body of her son was returned to her in Pays Plat. In her letter
she said a witness told her that her son had been made to
"scrub floors while ill with the measles and he wasn't given
any medical treatment." Bennett wrote back, "Your son was
made to wash floors as part of his regular school duties. You
can be pleased that the school is kept clean and sanitary."

I put the letter down. How did that mother feel getting this letter? Knowing that her child died in a place far
away, from a disease he had no resistance to, and that he
died scrubbing floors to keep the Christian school clean and
sanitary.

I looked at the painting of Nakina. So much I never asked. *Did you get measles? Do you remember your family? Did they make you scrub the floors clean for Jesus?*

———◈———

I decided to have a bath, which is a big flippin deal in the bush. Took all day. I started first thing in the morning. Snowshoed to the sauna with load after load of wood. I stoked the fire and kept filling the tank with snow. By afternoon the sauna was getting warm and the tank was almost full of water.

By the time the sun went down it was time to strip. In the narrow dressing room at the front of the sauna I took off my fur coat. I kicked off my boots and socks and felt the cold rough wood under my feet. I took off my overalls and flannel shirt, then undid my long johns and slid out of them. Naked. I ran my hand across my warm skin. My flesh. Old friend. Hadn't seen my body in months.

I opened the door of the sauna and the heat almost knocked me back. I tried to sit on the top bench but it was too hot—I couldn't breathe. The iron stove glowed red with the heat. I sat on the bottom bench and splashed a ladle of water from the tank across the rocks. A hiss of steam filled the room. I hung my head and felt water trickle down my neck. I poured more water on the rocks and moved up to the top bench. I took the birch switch hanging on the wall and slapped my shoulders and back. I could smell the sweet birch oil from the leaves. I slapped my feet and legs and ran the switch along my arms. The branches tickled.

It was too hot to breathe so I stepped out of the sauna

and walked barefoot along the snowy path. I stood naked under the stars, looking up at the Milky Way. I raised my arms to the sky and could see steam rising like smoke off my hot flesh. I stood on the snow with feet bare but felt no cold. I stood there five, maybe ten minutes, naked in a field of snow under the stars, in a perfect state of grace.

After a time the snow grew cold under my feet so I went back into the sauna. I lathered with birch soap and rinsed, then bundled up my clothes, slipped my bare feet into my boots and pulled the plucked beaver coat over my naked shoulders. When I got into the house I put on clean long johns and socks and wrapped my hair in a towel. I crawled into bed and fell into the long perfect sleep of the gods.

I started to ski every day. I went along the logging road back into the bush. It was still probably forty or fifty below but I could feel some heat in the sun when it reflected off the snow. The bush was silent. There was just the swish, swish, swish of my skis and little pings as I placed my poles.

Sometimes I stopped and stood under the trees. I saw deer. They got spooked if I was moving, but when I was still they'd walk up to me and around me. Sometimes I went so far into the bush that it was dark by the time I turned back. I kept supplies in my backpack—food, flashlights and duct tape. I taped the flashlights onto the top of my forearms and when my arms swung up and down, two long beams of light marked the path.

I came across a deer carcass one day. Wolves had taken it down and were circled around the kill. When they saw me they scattered, but before the last one bolted back into the bush he turned his face and I could see bright red blood dripping over his muzzle like a grin. Then they were gone and all that was left was a carcass ripped open—steam rising from the blood-red guts. I thought about the day Nakina and I watched Bernie Olfson slice open the belly of a moose on his front lawn. I turned and skied home.

chapter fifteen

One day I was tired of exploring the bush behind the house and decided to head down the road to see if I could find any signs of life. It was a sunny day and the snow was perfect for skiing, not sticky or slow. About five miles along the road I saw a house. Big two-storey house with a truck and a VW van in the driveway. I stopped in front of the house and thought maybe I'd just turn around and go back. I didn't really want to talk to anyone. Hadn't in months, but hell, I'd come all that way so I skied down the driveway and knocked at the door.

A woman, who looked to be in her twenties, opened the door and waved me in like she'd been expecting me. She was shorter than me and heavy-set and was wearing a long tie-dyed skirt with a plaid shirt over it. She looked down at the cross-country boots on my feet. "You skied here?"

"Yeah."

"Come on in. I just made tea."

I followed her into the house, through a narrow hallway

filled with coats and boots, into a large living room. There wasn't any furniture in the room except for a few mattresses on the floor that were covered with bright tie-dyed cotton blankets. As I followed her to the kitchen I saw a poster on the wall—a tree with roots deep in the ground and farther up, the tree morphed into the shape of a woman and this naked guy was fucking her—fucking a knot in the trunk of the tree woman.

I had two thoughts. First, this sure as hell wasn't a Finlander's house. And second, you really shouldn't fuck with Mother Nature.

"I'm Rita and this is Celeste." A small kid about five years old with short black hair sat at the table drawing.

"Hi, Celeste." The kid didn't answer or look up.

I sat down beside her and Rita brought over a mug of tea. I was a bit freaked out being around people, but Rita seemed OK and Celeste just kept drawing. Rita had soft blue eyes and blond hair pulled back into a long braid. The kid didn't look like her.

"You live close?" she asked.

"Down the Silver Falls Road about five miles."

"Near the highway?"

"No, the other way, down where the road turns. My place is a mile or so down the logging road."

"I didn't know anyone lived back there."

"No one does. Just me."

"Does the township plough that road?"

"They do, right up to my mailbox."

Rita put a bowl of vegetable stew in front of Celeste and me. It was good and I was thinking it had been a long time since I'd eaten any vegetables.

I looked at the picture the girl was drawing. "Is that your house?"

"My house in Africa."

"Did you live in Africa?"

"No, not yet. Want to draw?"

"Sure."

Celeste pushed some paper in front of me and moved her box of crayons between us. As we drew, two more people came into the kitchen: Tom, with beard and pipe and serious eyes, and Mary, with babe in arms. Mary sat down beside me, slipped the shoulder of her cotton blouse down and put the baby to her breast.

"There's stew in the pot. Help yourself," Rita said.

I continued drawing but looked up when one more guy walked in. His name was Frank and he dropped heavily into a chair across from me. He had wide shoulders, a broad barrel chest and a moustache that made him look like Charles Bronson. He stretched out one of his legs, rolled up the pant leg and snapped off a shiny pink plastic prosthesis. He laid the plastic leg against the table. People around the table kept talking, and no one seemed to think it was weird that some guy just sat down and snapped his leg off. I was glad Celeste had given me the paper. I put my head down and kept drawing.

Another guy came down the stairs and sat across from me. When I looked up I thought, "Jesus Christ." I mean really — Jesus Christ. He had long blond hair and a long beard and looked like those pictures of Jesus in my Sunday school book.

Actually, with his round wire-rim glasses he looked kind of like John Lennon too. Rita called him Lars and put a bowl of stew in front of him.

"I've got the plans for the house." Tom took the pipe out of his mouth to speak, but his voice was so low I could hardly hear him.

"When do you start building?" Rita asked.

"Spring. Not this spring, next."

"Log?" Rita asked.

"Yeah."

"So where do you get the logs?" Frank asked.

"Cut them."

"Yourself?"

"Yeah."

"How many?" Frank asked.

Tom took a deep draw on his pipe and looked up at the ceiling as if the answer were written there. "About forty-eight, maybe more."

"You're nuts. Where are you going to get all those logs?"

"I'll cut them from the edge of the clearing. Have to cut them, strip them and let them dry out for a year so they don't shrink."

"Don't be an idiot," Frank said. "Just get them hauled in. Do you even have enough on the property?"

"We'll see. I'm leaving next week to go up north."

"What for?"

"Got a job in Kirkland Lake. Noranda mine."

Mary looked up from the baby with a worried look. "When did you decide to take that job?"

"Last night. We need the money. Even if we cut the logs ourselves there's still the roof and windows. We need cash."

"Yeah, maybe but jee-zuz Tom, Kirkland Lake?" said Mary.

"Good money."

I looked down at my drawing and pretended I wasn't listening, but I was trying to put it all together. Looked like Tom and Mary were together so the baby must be his. I wondered who Celeste's dad was—if he was one of the men here. Frank seemed to fit in, but Lars was different. He was quiet and seemed to be watching everyone. Like I was.

Frank leaned across Tom's drawings and scratched his chin. "Bay window?"

"Mary's idea." Tom said.

"I want to be able to look down at the creek," Mary explained.

"Still, that's a big freakin window," Frank said. "Hard to keep the heat in with a window like that."

"I don't want to be stuck in a box in the middle of the bush with no windows," Mary said.

Frank leaned back in his chair till I thought it would topple over. "Yeah, well you'll change your mind next winter when you're freezing your fuckin nuts off."

Tom puffed on his pipe and said nothing. Someone put a record on in another room and I suddenly realized they had electricity. Don't know why I didn't notice that earlier. I mean refrigerator, electric lights, stereo—didn't take a genius to see they had power. There was a woodstove in the kitchen though.

"You heat with wood?" I asked.

"Oil mostly," Rita said. "There's a space heater in the other room. I like to cook on wood though. What about you?"

"Wood. I heat with wood."

I was amazed at how Celeste could close out everyone in

the room. She was drawing a long low house with a straw roof that sat in an open field. There were two elephants at the edge of the picture.

"I like that. It's really good," I whispered to her. I didn't want to break her concentration.

"No, it's not. I don't have brown. I need a brown crayon."

"Do you ever use paint?"

"I just have crayons."

"I could bring you some watercolour paint. Then you could mix the right colour."

She thought awhile before she replied. "I think that would be good."

I left as soon as I finished my stew. I thanked Rita for the food and she told me to come back any time.

When I was outside I realized that no one except Rita seemed to notice me leaving. As I skied down the driveway I saw there was a sign on the mailbox—it said Cripple Creek Farm.

I went back the next week with watercolour paints and brushes. There were more people there and I couldn't keep them all straight. Probably didn't matter. I figured they must be used to people coming and going all the time.

Frank was lying on one of the mattresses in the front room reading Milton Acorn out loud. His artificial leg was on the floor beside him, and I could see his stump, wrapped in a tensor bandage, just a few inches below his bent knee. His voice was deep and rough. "In the elephant's five-pound brain the whole world's both table and shithouse." He put the book down. "Fuckin amazing." He started to read aloud again to no one in particular.

Rita was in the kitchen at the woodstove stirring a big pot of something.

"Hi, I brought the paints for Celeste."

"She's upstairs. Go on up."

On the way up the stairs I pushed past Tom coming down, pipe still in his mouth. At the top of the stairs there were four doors. I stood listening. I don't know what I was listening for—the sound of Celeste drawing? I opened one door a crack and saw two bodies moving around like a clump of clay on a pottery wheel. I closed the door and was about to go back downstairs when I noticed a curtain at the end of the hall. Celeste was inside stretched out on the floor building a castle with wooden blocks. The baby was asleep in a crib against the wall.

"I brought you the watercolour paints," I said.

"I know. You said you would."

"Do you have some paper?"

Celeste went to a shelf of wooden crates under the window and came back with a stack of paper. We sat cross-legged on the floor and painted for an hour or more. She was drawing the house again. Said it was her house in Africa and she was going to live there because it was hot and she wouldn't ever be cold again like she was in this house.

"What's that big box in the front of the house?"

"It's for food for the lions and elephants who are going to visit me," she said.

"Oh."

"They won't want to come inside the house so I will feed them outside."

"I think they'll like that."

"And monkeys too. And maybe giraffes."

"What will you feed the giraffes?"

Celeste didn't answer but she started to draw something in the branches of a tall tree."

"What is that?"

"A table."

"In the tree?"

"Yes. I will climb up in the tree and put food on the table for the giraffes."

"Good idea." When I looked up I saw Rita standing in the doorway looking at Celeste.

She was smiling. "Hey, honey." She sat down on the floor and gathered her daughter into her arms. "I love your drawing. What's that in the tree?

"That's a table for the giraffe."

"My clever girl," she said, kissing Celeste on the forehead.

"I'm going to draw a zebra for you. Because it's your favourite."

"Beautiful." Rita nuzzled her face in Celeste's hair and they sat cuddling. "Stay for supper, Molly."

"Thanks, but I have to ski back before dark." I looked outside and saw the sun was setting. "I should head back now."

"I'll drive you back later. Stay. I'm making spaghetti."

I didn't want to stay. But I didn't want to go either. I liked being in the warm house with the smell of food wafting through the rooms. I liked painting with Celeste and I was starting to like being around people. "OK, thanks." I said.

Shortly after that the baby woke up howling. Mary came up to get him and told us supper was ready. When we were packing up the paints Celeste handed me her drawing. "That's for you Molly. Put it up on your wall."

"I will."

"You can come to Africa with me."

"I'd like that."

"I can't go now."

"No, but when you do I'll come to visit you."

Downstairs in the kitchen Mary was nursing the baby. The table was full. I noticed Frank had his leg back on. I sat down between Celeste and Lars.

There was a pot of spaghetti and garlic bread and salad. Bottle after bottle of wine was opened and joints were rolled and passed around. The room was hot with bodies and steam from the pasta and smoke from the joints, and my face felt flushed from the heat and the wine. Someone put on a record. The Band.

Lars turned to me. "Where you from?"

"Fort McKay. You?"

"Nipigon."

"So Jesus Christ is alive and well and living in Nipigon." Lars laughed.

"Are you a Finlander?" I asked.

"Swede."

"Do you live here?"

"No, just hanging out for awhile."

"Is that your guitar?" I could see a guitar lying against the wall behind him.

"Yeah." After dinner he played a few of his own songs on the guitar and he was good. Later, when Rita was about to drive me home, Lars took the keys from her hand. We didn't talk on the ride to my place, but it was comfortable. Before he drove off he said, "We're having a party on Friday. Send off for Tom. Come."

"I'm not sure."

"I'll pick you up."

I thought for a moment. I was really starting to enjoy my time at Cripple Creek Farm. "OK," I said.

chapter sixteen

was working on a new painting of Nakina. From a photo I'd taken the day we'd been out in the boat with Dad, with her hair blowing across her face and the water blue behind her. I was sketching out her profile. Long straight nose and high cheekbones. Her lips were open slightly. She had a strong chin. I don't think I'd noticed that before. A straight line from her jaw, which angled to a strong squared chin. The chin slightly prominent. A look of determination.

After a while I took a break and sat at the table reading through more of the papers from the school. A report from the Deputy Superintendent of Indian Affairs:

I submit the following report from my visit to the St. Mary's Residential School in Fort McKay Ontario, July 16, 1936.

Curriculum—The school is working to prepare the students for positions in domestic service and farming. I was witness to the students attending to their chores inside the school and was impressed with the high standards of cleanliness. Girls are given training in home economics, including meal preparation and kitchen hygiene. I observed boys in the school gardens where they were taught crop cultivation.

Rooms—classrooms, dining rooms, recreation rooms, sleeping dormitories all scrupulously clean

Dress—neat and clean in dress and appearance. Apparently happy and well nourished. I took lunch with the Archbishop and was presented with a good meal consisting of roast of beef, potatoes and vegetables from the school garden.

I put the report down. I remembered one morning when my dad had made porridge for breakfast and Nakina refused to eat it. Said the nuns made them eat cold porridge every morning at the residential school. They called it gruel, and sometimes it had bugs in it.

I looked at the report again. I doubted if any of the kids at the school that day were fed a nice meal of roast beef and potatoes like the superintendent was.

Another letter from 1949 was sent to the Department of Indian Affairs from a priest in the Fort McKay parish. Father Morrow gave the department authority to pick up three children, Joseph, Raymond and Paul Jackpine, from Perrault Falls. "The three children," said Father Morrow, "can be picked up as early as possible for enrollment at St. Mary's Residential School. The older boy Joseph is nine years of age, and his brother Raymond is eight years of age. The youngest child, Paul, is the illegitimate child of Rebecca Jackpine, the mother, who is an individual of low mentality.

The father, Frank Jackpine, I am told, does not want the children. It is a common finding that Indian parents have no interest in raising their own children and so it is in their best interest to be enrolled at the school."

I crumpled the letter in my hands. More god-damned government propaganda to justify the stealing of children.

I looked up at my first painting of Nakina, in the Lorna Doone. Nakina bent forward. Looking distant and worried. I stood up and grabbed a brush. I painted out her head and shoulders with white paint, and then, working fast, I painted her shoulders an inch higher, more rounded, heavier. I curved the neck so her head hung lower. That was it. I had caught Nakina in a rare moment when she didn't know she was being watched. A moment when I could see the weight of worry pressing down on her.

Lars arrived the following Friday and I invited him in.

"These yours?" He was looking at the paintings on the windowsill.

"I'm just playing around."

"I like it. That's First Avenue?"

"Yeah."

"And Mary Christmas. I like the red lips."

"Really."

"Yeah. Beautiful. Who's this?"

"My friend."

"At the Lorna Doone?"

"It's not finished. Still trying to get the face right."

"Hey, let me help with that." I was struggling to get my arm into the plucked beaver coat and Lars held it up for me.

"Thanks. I don't have anything to bring to the party. Is that OK?"

"Don't worry about it. Rita has a ton of food cooking and Frank and I did a beer run this morning."

Lars stood in front of the painting of Nakina. Finally he turned to me and said, "It's good."

We talked a bit in the car, about painting and music and writing songs. Lars turned on the radio. It was comfortable talking with him.

"Where is she now?" he asked when we were heading down the Silver Falls Road.

"Who?"

"Your friend. The one in the painting."

"I don't know."

"She move away?"

"Maybe. I'm not sure." The truth was I had been thinking about Nakina all week—wondering if there was any way I could send her a letter. I didn't know what I'd say. I just wanted to know where she was.

When we got to Cripple Creek the house was rocking. People were dancing to Moody Blues in the front room, and a couple were making out on the mattress under the "Don't fuck with Mother Nature" poster. In the kitchen Rita and Mary were cooking. Mary came over and dropped her sleeping baby into my arms. "Glad you made it. Have some wine."

Kid in one arm, wine in the other, I sat down and watched the women roll out perogy dough across the table. They had their hair tied back with kerchiefs like the ladies at the Polish legion.

I didn't like babies. Didn't know what to do with them. "What's the kid's name?" I asked.

"Blue."

"His name is Blue?" I asked.

"Yeah, Tom said he had this blue aura when he was born and that it was a sign."

"A sign of what?"

"A sign that his name was Blue."

I was thinking maybe he was blue because he wasn't getting enough oxygen and they should have called him Oxygen.

"He was born right out there." She was pointing to the mattress on the floor where the two people were making out.

Rita stopped cooking and wiped her hands on her apron. "It was amazing. We were all sitting on the floor massaging Mary's belly and she was screaming and we were screaming with her. It was like we all birthed Blue together, like one big womb pushing him out."

I wanted to wipe that happy image out of my head so I headed upstairs to see if I could find Celeste. She was in her room drawing. She seemed glad to see me. I put Blue down in the crib and he didn't wake up. He seemed like a pretty easygoing kid, which was a good thing for him.

We drew for a while and then Celeste asked me to read to her.

"Sure, what do you want me to read?"

Celeste handed me a copy of *Zen and the Art of Motorcycle Maintenance*.

"You're kidding."

"No I'm not."

She wasn't either. Man, she was a straight ahead kid.

I lay down on the mattress and read to Celeste. She put her head on my chest and looked up at the ceiling. After a while I noticed things were getting louder and crazier downstairs. I could smell perogies frying in onions. Jimmy Hendrix was belting out "Purple Haze" and the air was thick with pot. It was nice lying there reading and after a while we both fell asleep.

A while later baby Blue woke us with his crying. That kid had good lungs on him. I picked him up, and Celeste and I went downstairs. In the kitchen I handed Blue to his mother and lined up at the stove with my plate. As I was standing there I looked back to see if I could spot Lars. He was in the living room talking to Frank.

When I got my food I moved into the front room and sat down on a mattress on the floor beside Frank. He had his artificial leg on and his legs were spread straight out in front of him. Frank was really wasted. His shirt was open and he was eating his cabbage rolls with his hands, tomato sauce dripping down his bare chest. Frank and Lars were having a heated discussion about whether Neil Young wrote the song "Helpless" about Fort McKay. Frank said no, and Lars said yes and what did Frank know anyway—he was a Yank.

To change the subject I asked Frank what he did.

"I'm a prosthetician," he said.

I looked at Frank and he could tell from my stunned expression I didn't know what the hell he was talking about.

"I make artificial limbs. A prosthetician."

I don't know if it was the wine or the pot or both, but the word prosthetician set me off laughing. Between gasps for air I kept saying "pros-the-tician!"

Lars grabbed my plate and said he'd get me more perogies before they were all gone. Frank picked up a book and started reading poems about gods and dogs and dogs and gods, and it occurred to me that dog is god spelled backwards. When Frank started to read a Milton Acorn poem about flying foreskins I went back into the kitchen looking for Lars.

"Draft Dodger Rag" was playing on the stereo. Seemed appropriate. All the guys at Cripple Creek Farm were dodging the war in Vietnam. Everyone except Lars.

Lars handed me a plate of perogies and headed out the back door. Out the kitchen window I saw him walking across the field towards the sauna. He walked past Tom, who was talking to some skinny dude with a brush cut, who was waving a book in the air like he was some sort of southern Baptist preacher. Tom seemed angry and I could hear the skinny dude shouting but I couldn't hear what they were saying.

"Who's that?" I asked Rita.

"Who? Oh Sid. Friend of Tom's."

"Some friend."

Rita turned and looked out the window. Sid was still flailing the book around in front of Tom's face. "Yeah, bit of an asshole."

About an hour later Lars was back. "I got the sauna stoked, it's almost ready. Get your coat."

When I came back he took my hand and led me outside and down a path to the sauna. Lars stripped right away but I was shy. He handed me a towel and I wrapped it around myself and slipped my clothes off underneath. Lars threw water on the rocks and steam filled the room. We moved up to the middle bench.

Lars lifted the hair from the back of my neck and rubbed my shoulders with birch leaves. Moments later the door of the sauna opened and more people poured in. More hot wet naked bodies scrunched together along the lower bench. Lars and I moved up to the top bench to make room. He put his arm around me and his long hair fell across my shoulder.

Walking back to the house after the sauna I told Lars I had to get back to my house to stoke the fire and he took the keys to Rita's truck and drove me home. We didn't speak in the car but when we got to my house he leaned down, kissed me on the forehead and said he'd see me soon.

chapter seventeen

The next morning I stoked the fire and put a pot of water on the stove. There was frost on the inside of the window and it took hours for the kitchen to warm up. While I waited for the water to boil I looked through some of the photos from the residential school. Two photos side by side. On the left a boy about eight with straight black hair that came down to his shoulders. He was wearing a plaid shirt and jeans and was smiling at the camera. The second photo, on the right, the same boy with his hair cut short wearing a white shirt and black pants. In this photo he looked at the camera, or the person holding the camera, with an expression of distrust. Fear? I held the photocopy up in front of me. Someone had taped the two original images together. The nuns? Perhaps to show how much progress they'd made—every trace of Indian scrubbed clean.

That afternoon I skied to Cripple Creek. Lars was gone. "When did he go?" I asked.

"This morning," Rita said. "Frank drove him into town.

Got a call this morning from his mom. His dad fell and broke his arm and they needed Lars to come home and help out. They run a gas station in Nipigon and his dad can't work with his arm out of commission."

"Will he be coming back?"

"Maybe, but probably not for a couple of months at least."

I didn't stay long that afternoon. When I got home I put more wood on the fire and pulled the easel over to the window. I worked on the original painting of Nakina.

The next day I was painting the light on the window of the Lorna Doone and that's when I saw it. My reflection. Taking the photograph outside the restaurant that day I had captured my own reflection in the glass. Me, outside the Doone, camera held up in front of my face, taking a photo of Nakina sitting alone in the booth. That was it. It wasn't just Nakina sitting there, it was me outside, separated by glass, watching her. Nakina sitting alone, looking worried and vulnerable—not knowing I was watching her.

That was the story. I painted my reflection into the picture. It was hard work and I kept at the painting for the rest of the week. Me, observing Nakina through glass. Watching her but never getting close. That was how it felt now.

One day when the sun had some heat in it I skied down to Cripple Creek. There were more cars than usual parked out front.

"Hey, Molly. I'm glad you're here. Celeste has been looking for you." Rita was in the kitchen as usual, cooking for the men.

I sat down at the table and she put a mug of tea in front of me.

"Celeste wants you to teach her how to cross country ski. I found skis and boots for her in the attic."

"OK."

"Where have you been all week?"

"Just working on some paintings."

"I'd like to see them sometime."

"Sure." I could hear Blue hollering upstairs.

"I think he's cutting teeth. Mary's been up all night."

Frank walked through and gave me a nod. I felt like I was becoming part of the Cripple Creek landscape. I looked around for Lars but there was no sign of him.

"Molly, I got a pair of skis!" Celeste ran into the kitchen grinning from ear to ear. I'd never seen her face light up like that before. "Can you show me how to ski?"

"Wait a bit dear. Molly just got here. She's probably tired."

"No, I'm not. Let's go." I gulped back the warm tea and headed to the door to put my boots back on. Celeste sat on a wooden milk crate and I laced her ski boots.

Outside I helped her snap down the harness and tie the leather strap. "Now just slide your foot forward, like you're walking."

"Like this?"

"Perfect. And when your left foot is forward, put your right pole out. Good, that's it. Now slide your right foot forward. OK, now change hands. That's it. Plant your left pole."

"I'm doing it!" Celeste took a few strokes, then fell to the left into the deep snow. I helped her up.

"Now, just follow me. I'm going to cut a trail across this field. We'll go over by the beaver dam and then circle back."

I started off slowly and I could hear the swish of Celeste's skis behind me. Half way across the field I heard a shout, then the clacking of skis as she fell again.

I turned to help her up and she was laughing so hard I fell over on top of her, making her laugh even more. Once we got up on our feet we headed back to the house. I figured that was enough for one day.

"I did it, Mom! I was good, wasn't I Molly?"

"She's a natural. Maybe next time I'll take you out past the beaver pond."

Rita had made a banana loaf and she cut me a thick piece, still warm from the oven. I spent the afternoon drawing with Celeste. I should have headed home. I had started work on a new painting—the basket man—but I didn't feel like being alone so I stayed at Cripple Creek. The sun was low when I left. I taped the flashlights onto my wrists. By the time I got home I was following the ridge of light from the full moon. The stove was almost out and I spent the rest of the evening stoking it until the kitchen was warm enough so I could take off my fur coat.

Life in the bush seemed like one long fight against the cold. Heating the house, chipping ice off the washbasin in the morning, filling the wood basket, heating water on the stove for tea. There wasn't much time for anything else.

The basket man. I didn't know much about him, just that when I was growing up he would come down our street pushing a baby carriage filled with his baskets. He had bells on the carriage to let people know he was there. Mom bought a few baskets from him. Willow. He wove them mixing together red strips, which had the bark still on, and white strips, with the bark peeled off. The basket we'd had in our living room was deep and round with a tall handle. As I worked on the painting it bothered me that I didn't know anything about him. Was he married? Did he have children? Was he born in Fort McKay or did he come from somewhere else? Why did he weave baskets? To me he was just the short, dark-skinned man who appeared mysteriously on our street to sell his wares.

The next time I went to Cripple Creek, Celeste and I headed into the field again. This time we made it past the beaver pond and across the meadow behind the house. Rita had packed us sandwiches and we stopped at the edge of the clearing for lunch.

"You're doing great, Celeste."

"Can we ski to your house some day?"

"Maybe some day. It's pretty far. Maybe your mom could drive you."

"How about today?"

"I don't know. We'll have to ask her when we get back."

Back at the house a few people had gathered in the living room to play music. There was a woman I'd never seen before tuning a fiddle and a guy with a guitar. Celeste was tired after the long trek and she curled up with her head on my lap. Her little body felt warm.

Frank sat down beside us.

"So how's things in the prosthetics biz?"

"Can't complain."

"Where do you work anyway?"

"St. Joseph's Hospital, in the rehab wing."

"Do you go in every day?"

"Three times a week. I do a lot of the work here though. I've got a workshop in the barn."

"Hey, do you think you could pick up some stuff for me in town?"

"Sure. Make a list," Frank said as he finished rolling a joint.

I went into the kitchen and got some paper to make a list for Frank. I needed more canvases and paint and some canned goods and milk. I was getting low on food.

"Staying for supper?" Rita asked.

"I have to get back. It's late."

"Don't go back. You should stay here tonight."

"No, can't let the fire go out."

"OK, I'll drive you."

"Can I go too?" Celeste woke up and was rubbing her eyes. "I want to see where Molly lives."

"I guess so."

When we got to my place Rita and Celeste came in. It seemed strange to have people in my house. I lit the Coleman lamps.

"Did you paint this, Molly?" Rita asked.

"I did."

"It's good. Who is it?"

"It's my friend Nakina."

"There's my drawing!" Celeste spotted the drawing of her house in Africa that I had put up on the wall.

"It keeps me warm in this cold kitchen," I said.

I showed Celeste my bedroom and the pantry, and she had lots of questions about the house and who lived there with me and who had lived there before. She was a curious kid.

"Where is your mom and dad?" she asked

I was so surprised I didn't answer right away. "They died. They were in a car accident and they died."

"That's too bad. My dad died too. He died in Vietnam."

"I'm really sorry."

"That's OK. It was a long time ago."

Celeste looked at her mom and asked, "Can Molly come and live with us?"

"That's very sweet," I said, "but I'm OK here."

As I watched them getting into the truck I thought maybe one day I'd invite Celeste to come and paint with me.

chapter eighteen

n the boxes of papers from the residential school I found some correspondence from 1950 between the school superintendent and the Department of Indian Affairs. Letters explaining how to trick parents into signing the needed documents. They told the priests to take a doctor with them to examine the kids, then get the parents to sign the permission forms thinking they were signing medical papers. It worked. A letter from the school superintendent in 1951 boasted that the school was full—more than a hundred kids.

There were journals going back years with entries for each student under the headings of age, name, age on admission, place of birth, name of parents. The first column gave the number that was assigned to each child. I looked down the column of age on admission—some children were as young as four or five. Children the same age as Celeste were taken away from their families, their communities, their culture.

I wondered if Nakina knew what year she'd been taken

to the residential school. Maybe I could find a journal with her registration in it—with her parents' names and where she was born. Under the chart of admissions for each year was a chart for discharge of pupils. Under reasons for discharge I saw that some of the children had been taken to the sanatorium. Tuberculosis. Some were listed as deceased. I wondered if their bodies were sent home and if not where they were.

I had photocopied lots of photos. A photo of a boy having his head shaved by a nun. A photo of a room full of metal beds and kids in striped pajamas kneeling beside the beds, praying. Two nuns stood beside the door. The striped pajamas reminded me of the movie about the concentration camps.

Another photo had been taken outside the school. Twelve nuns and three priests stood on the school stairs. In four long lines in front of the steps were the students. Maybe a hundred of them. All of the girls had their black hair cut in the same bob, just below their ears with straight bangs. They all wore uniforms. The girls were in white blouses and black jumpers, and the boys wore shirts and black pants. All scrubbed and clean and white. Red kids in, white kids out. Just like Nakina said.

I remembered her telling me that the nuns shaved her head when she got there and put something on her scalp that burned. She told me that they beat her when she spoke Ojibwe.

She didn't tell me much. But then, I didn't ask.

I found a letter from a Sister Bernadette addressed to the Abbess of St. Mary's. It was a letter of resignation:

Dear Reverend Mother,

After long and difficult consideration I have decided to renounce my vows and therefore will no longer continue in service as a teacher at St. Mary's school. I took my call to serve God with great conviction, but cannot in good faith continue to teach the children in my care because I believe the rules and punishments handed to the children are cruel and harmful. I am instructed that if a child speaks in his native language he must take his fingers and pull his tongue out of his mouth and stand this way for hours to show the other children the consequences of not speaking English. I have seen children faint and fall to the floor after hours of standing in this way. I cannot believe such treatment is right in the eyes of God. I believed my calling was to bring these children to the word of God, but if the very church that brings these children to God also causes them harm, will that not destroy their faith?

I wondered what had happened to Sister Bernadette after she left the church. Did she ever teach again? Was her letter ever read, or was it just hidden away in these files?

There was a letter dated 1958 from the school superintendent to the father of Richard Owbance:

I have received your letter dated March 3rd containing allegations that your son, Richard Owbance, was mistreated while in residence at St. Mary's. I can assure you that the allegations your son has made regarding Father Martin are completely unfounded. It is my understanding that he made these accusations in order to justify running away from the school. Leaving the school without permission is a serious offence and put your son at risk of harm. I must also inform you that your son is in violation of the Ontario Education Act. He must return to St. Mary's immediately, and if he fails to do so charges will be brought against you for interfering with the laws surrounding the education of your son.

Allegations against Father Martin. What allegations? What had he done? And if they were true, who would believe Richard's word against the priest?

Clipped to that letter was a letter from the school superintendent to the Department of Indian Affairs: "Regarding the letter from the father of Richard Owbance I can assure you that the allegations of mistreatment are completely unfounded. As for the boy being abused that is the usual line of the Indian. It is the same story over and over again. The Indian does not want to do what he is told or follow regulations so he makes false accusations. It must be impressed upon the Indian that he cannot have his own way in matters concerning the Department of Indian Affairs."

No protection. The children had no protection from harm. The state and church held all the power. I thought back to the movie about the holocaust. "Who amongst us will keep watch?" Who was watching over Richard Owbance? Over Nakina?

I got up, put on my coat and went outside. I walked out into the field past the sauna. I needed to get away—away from the papers from the residential school, from the painting, from Nakina staring at me. I had to think. There was so much I didn't know. So much I never asked. I should have asked. All that mattered now was that I missed her. I needed to know where she was and if she was OK. I went back into the house and wrote a letter.

Nakina,

I don't know if you are still at this address. A lot has happened. Tell me where you are.

Molly

I addressed the letter to the last address I had for her on Simpson Street, added my return address and a stamp, and then skied down to the sharp bend in the road where my mailbox was. I put the letter inside and raised the red flag.

The next morning I skied to the farm and asked Rita if Celeste could spend the afternoon with me. Celeste was excited, and before I skied home I invited Rita for dinner. When I got home I spent the rest of the morning cooking—something I wasn't very good at. I had a recipe for vegetarian chili and found tomatoes and kidney beans in the pantry.

Rita's truck arrived early that afternoon. Celeste brought her skis and a bag filled with drawing supplies. We had tea together, then Rita headed home.

"Do you want to ski up behind the house?" I asked Celeste.

"No, let's draw first."

"OK. Here, I have a canvas for you." I put a fresh canvas on the easel and pulled a chair up in front of it. "Here's a brush, and you can mix the colours on this board, like this."

"What are you going to do?" she asked.

"I'm going to sketch." I showed Celeste the sketching pad I had been working in.

"What is that?"

"A hand. I was trying to paint a hand and I couldn't get it right so I spent a few days drawing my own hand. See, I drew it open, then holding a pen. The more you look at something the more you can see."

"And what's this?"

"Frost. When it gets really cold the frost on the windows looks like feathers. I was drawing the patterns I saw in the frost."

Celeste started to paint. She used strong colours, reds and yellows, and her brush strokes were thick.

"What are you painting?" I asked.

"Summer."

"Nice."

We worked for a long time in silence, and it felt good to have company. After a while Celeste spoke.

"Molly, tell me about your mom and dad."

"Well, my dad worked at the mill. And he raced hydroplane boats. They look like flying saucers and go so fast they seem like they're flying across the top of the water. He was a really sweet guy.

"What was your mom like?"

"My mom was…" I thought about how to explain my mother—smart, sometimes sad. "She read a lot," I said, "like me."

"Do you miss them?"

"I do. Every day."

"I miss my dad sometimes. But I don't really remember him. I was little when he died."

"Was he a soldier?"

"No. He was a helicopter pilot. His helicopter got shot down. In Vietnam."

We painted for a couple of hours, and talked, and didn't talk. When we stopped I took Celeste's painting and hung it up on the kitchen wall beside the door.

"Looks good," I said.

"Not as good as yours. Some day you are going to be a famous artist."

I laughed and was about to tell her I wasn't any good, but her face was so serious, I just said, "Thanks, kid."

We went out skiing, and I took Celeste up the hill behind the north field and deep into the bush. We saw a deer and lots of rabbit tracks in the snow. When Rita arrived we were warming up in the kitchen with mugs of hot chocolate.

"Did you have a good time, sweetie?" Rita asked, kissing Celeste on the forehead.

"Look Mom, on the wall."

Rita turned to look at the painting. "You did that?"

"Molly helped me."

"It's called *Summer*," I said.

"What can I do to help?" Rita asked.

"Nothing. Just sit down and relax. I'm going to wait on you for a change."

"I don't mind."

"No really. You're always taking care of everyone else."

"Thanks." Celeste was curled up in Rita's lap and looked like she was going to sleep.

"She can have a nap in my room. Supper won't be ready for an hour or so," I said.

Rita carried Celeste into the bedroom and when she came back I opened one of the bottles of wine Toivo had given me. I'd been saving them for a special occasion.

"So Molly, how did you end up living out here on your own?" Rita asked.

"I had a friend who had a friend who was selling this place. Seemed like a good idea at the time."

"It's strange though, living out here alone."

"What about you? What brought you to Cripple Creek Farm?" I asked, changing the subject.

Rita laughed. "Seemed like a good idea at the time. We had plans, before Jamie got drafted. We were going to open a restaurant in Chicago. He was killed six months after going over to Vietnam and that changed everything. Then about a month after Jamie's funeral my brother Tom…"

"Tom is your brother?"

"Yeah."

"So Celeste and Blue are cousins?"

"Right. Well Tom got his draft notice, and he and Mary were expecting. So they decided to come to Canada. There wasn't any choice really. And Celeste and I decided to come with them."

"And Frank?"

"Tom and I have known him since we were kids. He was in Vietnam when Jamie was. In the marines. A land mine went off and he lost his leg. Anyway, when he came back and got out of rehab, he took a course in making artificial limbs and got a job at the hospital in Fort McKay. So we all moved here with him. What are you making?"

"Bannock. My friend Nakina taught me how to make it." I rubbed floury hands on my apron and pointed to a canvas leaning up against the wall. "That's Nakina."

"Ahh. Native?"

"Ojibwe. She spent a summer up on a northern reserve and learned how to make bannock. It's easy. Good with blueberries too. So you were going to start a restaurant?"

"Jamie was a fantastic cook. The plan was that when he got back from Vietnam we were going to use his army pension and some money his mom had given us to start the restaurant."

"But he didn't come back," I said.

"No. There was a pension, but I didn't want to do it without Jamie."

"So then you came to Cripple Creek."

"I wanted to keep an eye on my little brother, and it was hard living in the States. You couldn't forget about the war."

"Does Celeste like it here?"

"She misses home. She hates the cold. But I think she's happy most of the time. It's been hard."

"How do you mean?" I asked.

"Living in a place you don't belong, a place you didn't chose. I hope we can go home when the war is over. Who knows what will happen. But until then all I can do is try to get through the best way I can."

I thought about after my parents died when I had to move out of my home into a place I didn't chose with a family that wasn't mine.

"Maybe that's what we're all doing." I said. "Just trying our best."

chapter nineteen

I went back to Cripple Creek every day for the next few weeks. Celeste and I were skiing farther and farther along the road each day.

One afternoon after skiing I sat at the kitchen table warming my hands on a mug of hot chocolate. Rita was relaxing in the rocking chair with her feet up, reading a book.

"Got a letter from Lars today," she said.

"You did? So, what's happening?"

"His dad is doing better but still can't work, so Lars has to stay on for a while longer and help out at the garage. Hey, Celeste is still talking about the day she spent with you. You made a big impression on her."

"I'm glad. I had a great time too. I'd like to do it again soon." I looked outside and saw it was getting dark. "I think I'd better head back."

"Want a ride? It's late."

"No, I'm good. Thanks."

I taped my flashlights onto my arms before heading off as

the sun was setting. I didn't want to think as I skied home so I concentrated on the pattern of the skis—right swish, left swish, right swish, left swish—like a meditation.

I was pissed off. Why did he write to Rita and not to me? But what did I expect? I was such an idiot—right swish, left swish, right swish, stupid fuckin idiot, swish. When I was close to the turn in the road I could see that the flag of my mailbox was up. I put the flag down, reached inside, and when I pulled out the letter I saw it was the one I had sent to Nakina. Across the front was written, "Address unknown."

I didn't go back to Cripple Creek that week. Too cold to go outside, too cold to ski. I was glad to stay home. Frank came one afternoon and dropped off the supplies I'd asked him to get. I invited him in for tea but he said he had to get back.

I was almost finished the painting of the basket man and thought it was OK. It was black and white, like all the paintings, but I painted the bells on the baby carriage silver.

The frost on the windows was about an inch thick. I took a knife and scraped a small square so I could see the outside world. Not much to see. At night I made an extra trip out to the woodpile and filled the wood basket. I'd have to keep the stove stoked.

Maybe it was the cold snap, or maybe I was bored, but for that week I just wanted to sleep. I slept, woke up, stoked the stove and slept. Nights rolled into days rolled into nights, and my dreams seemed more real than being awake. I dreamt about Mom and Dad. Being out in the boat with Dad, flying across Lake Superior. Making apple pies in the kitchen with Mom, and I could smell the apples and cinnamon. Swimming at Loon Lake and Mom wrapping my shivering little body up in a towel. And when I woke up, for a few seconds I thought I was at home and Mom and Dad were sleeping in their room across the hall.

One night I woke and my frozen nose told me it was time to stoke the stove. I got up out of bed and headed into the kitchen. I stopped in the doorway. The kitchen was lit with a weird light. The window had a strange glow—like someone had painted a pink watercolour wash on the frost.

I was sleepy. I was cold. I fed wood into the fire, all the while looking back over my shoulder at the strange glow coming from the window. Fire stoked, I went to the window to see if I could peek out through the square I'd scraped in the frost, but it had frosted over again. I grabbed the plucked beaver coat, pulled on my fur hat and slipped my feet into my boots. The door didn't open right away. Frost had gotten into the latch. I pulled and pushed and wiggled and finally the door opened.

The sky was red. Northern lights. A bright red band of the aurora borealis over the tree line.

No. Maybe not northern lights. Not changing and fluid, just red.

Wolves howled and I turned. They were about twenty feet away up on the hill. I looked up at the sky. To the east it was black, and to the north, black. To the west, towards Cripple Creek, it was red. I wanted to go out to the barn and get the wooden ladder and climb up onto the porch roof to see if I could see anything above the tree line. But it was too cold. I learned my lesson before and I could already feel a tingling in my hands. I went back inside.

I kept waking up all night, stoking the stove. The pink feather patterns on the frosted window were fading. I thought about it and didn't think about it. Could have been a lot of things, and there was nothing I could do about it in the middle of the night in the middle of the bush.

When the sun came up I went into the kitchen and the frost on the window was white. I wondered if the red glow had been a dream. Hard to tell. I went outside and a pair of blue jays squawked at me from a pine tree. It was so cold my footsteps on the snow squeaked as loud as the blue jays. Bloody cold.

I stoked the stove, made some tea and started working on the painting of the Empire building with the clock tower. The building was red brick, built in 1935. It was hard to get the texture of the brick right.

Too cold to go out, I spent the day in a strange dreamy half-awake, half-asleep limbo. That night I was heating up a can of beans when I heard a vehicle coming down the road. I threw on my coat and opened the door, thinking it was probably Rita. It was a truck, but not Rita's. It was that skinny guy with a brush cut I'd seen at Cripple Creek the night of Tom's party. Sid.

I held the door open and he came into the house without speaking. He went directly to the stove and began to warm his hands.

"You heard?" he asked.

"Heard what?"

"About the fire."

"What fire?"

"Cripple Creek"

"What happened?" I asked, not wanting to hear his answer.

"Chimney fire."

I looked to see if I could read anything on his face. Nothing.

"Is everyone OK?"

"No."

I waited for him to say more. "Was someone hurt?" I didn't know why he was making me ask all the questions.

He turned to me, and in a cold, flat voice, said, "Blue and Celeste are dead."

My legs started shaking and I dropped into a chair. I looked up at Sid, unable to speak.

"Frank asked me to drive over and tell you. Blue and Celeste were sleeping upstairs. Rita and Frank were downstairs and I was out in the sauna with some people. The fire started in the attic and by the time they realized it they couldn't get up the stairs to the kids."

"Where was Mary?"

"In Kirkland Lake visiting Tom. Rita was taking care of Blue."

I closed my eyes and thought, "Ladybird, ladybird fly away home, your house is on fire, your children all gone." I couldn't move. I couldn't breathe. After a time the guy got up to leave.

"The funeral is Wednesday. Knox United Church. I'll come get you if you want."

I nodded.

"I'll come at nine."

"I don't have a clock." I could tell by the look on his face he thought I was an idiot so I just said, "I'll be ready."

When he left, I went into the bedroom, knelt down beside my bed and pulled out a suitcase of clothes I'd shoved under there when I moved to the house. I wanted to find something to wear to the funeral. Kneeling there I felt like I should pray, but all that came out was, "Fuck you! Fuck you! Fuck you!" I smashed my hands on the bed and kept screaming, "Fuck you!"

I was ready two days later when Sid came. He didn't talk on the drive in. I closed my eyes and listened to the hum of the truck engine. I hadn't been to Knox United since Mom and Dad died. I listened to the beating of the windshield wipers and tried not to think.

There was a line of people standing outside the church. As I went up the stairs Sid put his hand on my shoulder and guided me through a group of people standing near the door. We walked past the front lobby, where people were signing the memorial book, and went into the church. I put my head down. I didn't want to see. Some recorded organ music was playing somewhere.

When I opened my eyes I saw two small white coffins at the front of the chapel. There were daisies on the larger one and blue carnations on the little one. I could see Rita at the front. She was staring ahead and her face was like stone. There was an older man and woman on either side of her—her mom and dad. Mary sat on the other side of the church, bent forward. Tom was trying to hold her up. I saw Mary fall and Tom lift her up. He took her through the door to the left side of the chapel. I knew that door. It led to a private room where the family could fall apart without making a scene.

I felt tears coming and I knew I had to distract myself so I started to count. I had to count fast. Ten, twenty, thirty, forty. The minister was speaking, "Suffer the little children to come onto me," and I thought, why do you want the children to suffer? What the hell kind of god wants children to suffer? Ten plus ten is twenty, twenty plus twenty is forty, forty plus forty is eighty.

Frank was at the front, hands bandaged, talking about Celeste and Blue and I could hear sobs and Rita still didn't move. I counted the diamonds in the pattern in the carpet. When I got to fifty-eight I heard Bob Dylan's raspy voice from the speakers at the front of the chapel, "May god's blessing keep you always, may your wishes all come true."

I tried to count faster but tears were rising.

"May your heart always be joyful, may your song always be sung, and may you stay, forever young."

Two small white coffins were being carried out. Rita had fallen on the floor wailing, Dylan was wailing and I was wailing, and god I wanted my mom and dad so goddamned bad. I fell forward and felt an arm go around my shoulder. Sid pulled me against his chest and I burrowed my face into his jacket like my mom was holding me and telling me shush, honey shush, everything's going to be OK. Sid grabbed my arm and helped me out to the truck. I was still crying when the truck turned off the highway onto the Silver Falls Road. I leaned my head against the window and fell asleep.

———◆———

When we got to my house I followed him inside. He stoked the fire and then went outside and I could hear the ping of an axe splitting wood. I looked out the frosted window and could see the reflection of his arms rising and falling as he chopped.

He came back in with an armload of wood and dropped it in the wood box. He came across the room and put his hand on my shoulder and steered me to the bedroom as if it were his room and he were inviting me in. I let him. I let him take me into the bedroom and I let him undress me and I let him lie beside me. I let him wrap his arms around me because I wanted to be held and I let him come inside me because I needed to be loved.

chapter twenty

When I woke the next morning I heard chopping behind the house and when I went into the kitchen Sid came through the door with another armload of wood. "You should have had a proper woodpile ready in the fall. At least four cords."

"That's all that was cut when I moved in. It's enough."

He didn't say anything, just raised an eyebrow. A subtle gesture that said he knew he was right.

After the funeral he stayed. It was that simple. For weeks after the funeral I fell into a fog. I couldn't cry. I couldn't eat. I slept a lot. Slept and woke and slept and when I was awake I could hear him moving around in my house. I could smell pipe tobacco, and he brewed coffee but never offered me one. Finally I got out of bed and went into the kitchen.

My paintings were gone. The painting on the easel and the ones I had lined up on the windowsill. All gone. The papers from the residential school that I had put in piles on the kitchen table were gone.

"Where's my stuff?" My voice sounded thin and shaky.

"What? You mean those sketches?"

"My paintings."

"I put them out in the porch. I needed some space."

"I was working on them."

He looked at me as if to say he'd done me a favour by moving them.

I looked around to see if anything else had been changed. He had laid his books on the side table beside the chair. His chair. The alpha wolf pissing around the corners of my house.

"I'm hungry," I said and sat down at the table.

He went into the living room, sat down in the chair and started to read. I got up, opened a can of beans, warmed them on the stove and put out two plates of beans with bread.

When Sid sat down at the table he said, "You could use some extra insulation up in the attic."

"I'm warm enough."

"Wasting heat. You need to get some insulation up there and fix these windows."

I looked at him and thought about this stranger sneaking around my house while I was sleeping. How long had I been in bed? Weeks?

"There was a benefit dance in town. To raise money for Mary and Rita," he said.

"When?"

"Last week."

"Why didn't you tell me?"

He shrugged.

"For Christ's sake, why didn't you wake me?

"Don't get pissed off with me. You're the one who's been sleeping for weeks."

He went into the living room and I could hear him rustling through some stuff. He came back into the kitchen. "Don't you even have a goddam hammer in this place?" He was trying to build a small bookcase to go beside the chair.

I got him a hammer and some nails and wood from the barn. For a while the project kept him busy but after about an hour he started cursing and flung the hammer against the wall. I decided it was time to get out of the house and as I left I heard him shout, "If I had any decent tools I could…" I closed the door.

The weather was getting warmer, and every day I strapped on my skis and went deep into the bush. It felt good to be alone. Sid had a way of pushing at me, asking me questions, making me feel stupid.

"So how can you afford this place?" he asked one day.

"What do you mean?"

"Well, you're just a kid and you own this house and land. You do own this place, don't you?"

"Yeah. It's mine," I said.

"So, where'd you get the cash?"

"My parents. They died. They left some money."

"How much?"

"Why?"

"Just curious. If you've got some cash you should let me help you fix the place up."

"It doesn't need fixing."

"Yeah, well I had a look at your roof and…"

"It doesn't need fixing."

I was getting angry and that just seemed to set him off more. He kicked the porch door shut and I jumped. "Don't be so goddamned cheap," he said. "This place is falling down around you and you don't even care. And there's nothing to eat here. You need to go into town and buy some proper food."

I could feel his rage rising. I put on my coat and boots and headed outside again. Seemed like I was spending more time outside my house than in it.

When I went back Sid had papers scattered all over the table. He had made plans for tearing down the old chicken coop and building a shed for his motorcycle. I didn't say anything. Didn't want to start a fight.

The next morning he was dressed early. "I'm going into town."

I didn't know why he was telling me. I didn't expect him to stay.

"I'll be gone for about a week. I need to sort some stuff out."

I didn't say anything.

"I need some money for gas, and there's some stuff I need to get."

"I don't…"

"Look, I know you got cash here. Are you going to get it, or should I?"

I went into my room and got the money from my wallet, which was sitting on the dresser. He must have gone through it when I was sleeping. Knew what was there.

Sid left without speaking and after he was gone I could still feel him in the house. I could still smell him on my sheets, could hear his voice. I wondered how he had gotten into my house, into my bed and into my head. Like a rat skittering in through a crack in the wall.

By night the cold air had washed his scent away and it felt good to be alone again. I heard a lone wolf back in the hills. One solitary sad cry, silence, then a chorus of four or five. Their voices carried far on the night air.

The next morning I went to the porch and brought the canvases into the kitchen and set them up against the wall. There were eight finished paintings—three I was still struggling with. I brought my paints in from the porch and put them on the counter near the woodstove to warm them up. I poured a cup of tea and sat down to look at the paintings.

They weren't bad, but it was as if I could only get so far. I looked up on the wall at the painting Celeste had done. She was so confident when she painted. So sure of herself. I envied that. When she painted it was as if she could already see what she was going for—could see the final image. She picked up the brush and the creative force flowed through her without hesitation. I held back, unsure. It showed in my work. There was a certain competence in line and form, but something was missing that I saw in Celeste's painting. Joy. I looked at the thick brush strokes and vibrant colours of Celeste's *Summer* and I could feel the joy.

I walked to the easel, took down the painting I was working on and put up a fresh canvas. Without thinking, without hesitation, I took the brush and began to paint—angry streaks of red rage and black sorrowful strokes. Grief flowed through my brush.

That week I painted. And waited. Waited for Sid.

The day he arrived I was coming back from stoking the sauna. I was standing about ten feet from the house when his truck pulled into the driveway. I walked slowly forward, my heart pounding so fast I could feel it in my chest.

When he opened the truck door I was about three feet away.

"Give me a hand with this stuff."

I stood looking at him but said nothing. I didn't move. I put my hand in my pocket and felt the key to the door. Safe.

"I need some help. Grab those boxes." He was lifting a box from the back of the truck.

"No." It came out almost a whisper.

"What?" He turned to face me.

"I said no." Louder, but voice trembling.

"You're not going to help?"

Standing in front of him I was surprised at how short he was. Inside my house he seemed to take up so much space. I tried to speak but no words came out.

"Stop screwing around." Sid took the box and walked towards the front door.

He held the box with one arm and pulled the latch on the door. It was locked.

"You're kidding!" He threw the box on the ground and tried the door again. He looked up at the roof then back at me. "Come on, for Christ's sake—open it!" He grabbed the handle and tried to force the door.

I looked at him trying to break into my house, my home, and I could feel hairs rising on the back of my neck. Anger. I could feel it rush up into my chest like a fist.

"Get the fuck out of here!" I shouted.

Sid looked at me, shocked. He stood facing me for a few minutes and I wondered what he would do, if he would come at me. Then he picked up the box, walked back to the truck and threw it in the back. He slammed his fist against the truck. "Bitch!" He got into the truck and pulled out of the driveway so fast that he almost got stuck in the snow bank.

I stood watching until the taillights of the truck disappeared and my knees stopped shaking.

When I got back inside I sat down at the table, looked out the window, and with absolute certainty knew what I was going to do. I think I'd been moving towards it for years. Maybe Sid was the final kick in the ass, but the real reason for my decision was Celeste.

After the fire I ran away. I was good at running away, like the way I hid in bush after my parents died. It dulled the pain for a bit but in the end it didn't help. I owed Celeste more than that. She taught me so much and I didn't want to let her down, so I decided no more running. That day I sat down and began to fill out the forms for admission to the Nova Scotia College of Art and Design.

I had to prepare a portfolio of sketches, which wasn't a problem as I had been doing sketches all winter, working out some of the technical problems I had with the paintings. The hardest part was writing an essay about why I wanted to go to NSCAD. I'd start the essay, then throw it out because everything I wrote sounded stupid. I tried to think back to when I first wanted to go to art college. I remembered the day in 1968 when Nakina and I walked down First Avenue and I took the photos. Nakina asked me why I was taking them and I got pissed off with her—not because she asked the question but because I didn't have an answer.

Now I understood what I was trying to capture that day. When I looked through the lens everything stopped—and in that suspended moment everything, no matter how small or ordinary, seemed beautiful. Everything seemed important and connected and necessary. Every person mattered. The hands on the clock in the tower mattered. There was beauty in every bit of dirty snow piled up on the curb and beauty in the rubber galoshes the man from the hardware store was wearing. In stopping time I saw the layers that connected everything into a whole.

By May I had everything ready. I packed up the car but wasn't sure if the old girl would start because I hadn't driven it all winter. She didn't let me down, started right away. When I got to Anna's house Toivo answered the door and all he said was, "You're late."

"Yeah, no shit, a year late."

Kiiko was in the kitchen. She came out and gave me a hug, squeezed so hard it hurt my ribs, and said, "Make yourself useful and set the table."

And that was it. That's the thing about people in the north—no bullshit. I set the table and sat down. "I'm applying to go to NSCAD," I said.

"What's that?" Toivo asked.

"An art school. In Halifax."

"Halifax?" He said it like it was Timbuktu.

"Yeah. Don't know if I'll get in, but I'm going to apply."

Kiiko leaned across the table and put her hand on mine and smiled.

"Where's Anna?" I asked

"Writing exams. She'll be home late."

When Anna got home Toivo took us to the Wayland to celebrate. Nothing had changed and all the old gang was there.

"So, you're finished at Lunkhead?" I asked Anna.

"Almost, just one more exam."

"What next?"

"University of Manitoba. Going to do a law degree."

"Winnipeg. Never thought you'd move to the Peg."

"Never thought you'd move to Halifax."

"I haven't even sent my application in yet."

"So you got the bush out of your system?"

I laughed. "Maybe. I might go back some day. Hey, I sent a letter to Nakina."

"Did she write back?"

"No. The letter came back. She'd moved."

"Too bad," Anna said.

"You haven't seen her around, have you?"

"No, haven't seen her since she left high school."

"Hey, remember the night we came here after high school graduation?"

"Yeah, we got up and belted out that Johnny Cash song. Good times."

———◇———

I got everything together for the portfolio and once I sent it off to Halifax I headed back out to my house to wait. Driving home along the Silver Falls Road I thought about taking a detour past Cripple Creek Farm, but I couldn't do it. When I was in town I'd tried to find Rita, but she'd moved back to the States with her parents. Mary and Tom had moved north. Everyone scattered after the fire.

That summer I dug up a garden and planted potatoes and kale. I tried a few other things to see what would grow in the clay soil. The letter came in July. I was accepted. Had to read the letter four times before I could believe it. I had been certain I wouldn't get in. I drove into town that night to tell Kikko and Toivo.

At the end of August, Toivo and Kikko came out to help me dig up the garden. I left them with enough potatoes to get them through the winter. I left the house keys with Toivo. He drove me to the airport. I was nervous and kept checking my ticket and boarding pass and running to the bathroom to pee. I went over and over the instructions with Toivo about selling my car and shipping my stuff out by train once I got there.

"Yeah, yeah. I got it. I'll get the stuff to you, don't worry."

"The house will be pretty quiet now with Anna and me gone. " Anna had left for Winnipeg the week before.

"Yeah, about time. We'll finally get some peace and quiet."

"Admit it, you'll miss us," I teased.

"You better get on that plane if you're going. I haven't got all day to hang around here."

I threw my arms around Toivo, then turned quickly so he couldn't see my tears as I went through security.

Flying out of Fort McKay the plane banked over the Nor'Wester Mountains, then circled back over the city before heading out across Lake Superior. I looked down at the wharf in front of Sask Pool 7 and remembered the skinny little girl swinging her legs over the side of the dock. I looked down at First Avenue and the Empire Building and remembered standing on that street looking up at a plane flying overhead, thinking about all the lucky people getting out. Now it was *me* getting out. I thought I'd be excited, but I felt like I was stepping off a cliff—falling into the unknown.

As we lifted higher over the water I could see the profile of the Stone Man lying across the harbour with his arms crossed over his chest watching me fly out across Lake Superior. Away.

book three

chapter twenty-one

In some ways Halifax was a lot like Fort McKay. I lived not too far from the waterfront in a house on a hill and from my bedroom window I could see the harbour. It reminded me of Lake Superior. Halifax looked like Fort McKay but it was different. People were polite but kept to themselves because of the whole come-from-away thing. If you weren't born on the East Coast or didn't have family going back about ten generations you were considered a come-from-away. It wasn't something people came right out and said, just a thing that sat under the surface.

In Fort McKay if someone had a problem with you they just said it right to your face. People were more straight ahead that way. I missed that. I missed Toivo and Kiiko and Anna. I missed the bush and the Stone Man.

Toivo had shipped all my canvases out by train, and as I was unpacking them I unwrapped the painting of Nakina at the Lorna Doone restaurant and set it on the mantelpiece. I unwrapped tissue from around the tiny black shoe I had found in the rubble of the residential school and placed it on the mantelpiece beside the painting. I wondered if Nakina was still in Fort McKay. It felt so far away.

School was intense, which was good, so I didn't have much time to be homesick. I was taking a full course load, with art history, two drawing classes, constructed forms and photography. I signed up for a darkroom tutorial as well.

When I wasn't in class I wandered the streets of Halifax with my camera. I developed the photos myself and was learning a lot about how to use light to manipulate the images. I decided to use the photos to make note cards to send home.

October 18, 1972
Dear Toivo and Kiiko,

Hope you like the card. I took the photo on the front. It's the old clock on Citadel Hill which is about a five-minute walk from my place. It was built around 1800.

Happy Thanksgiving! Sorry I missed all the good grub. Did you make pumpkin pies?

I'll bet it was good to have Anna home for a visit. I got a letter from her last week and it sounds like she's doing OK. Things here are good. I'm still getting settled in and figuring things out. I like our house. It's an old house, built in the 1870s. You don't see many houses that old in Fort McKay! There's three bedrooms upstairs so we all get a room, and then a big kitchen, and the living room has a fireplace, which is nice because it's starting to get cold.

I know I told you I might come home for Christmas,

but I've decided to stay in Halifax. I have exams two weeks before Christmas and then I want to spend some time in my studio over the holidays to get ready for next term. Oh yeah, I have a studio. I share it with two other students, but it's a big space.

Molly

I wasn't completely honest about my reasons for not going home at Christmas. I was just starting to feel settled in Halifax, and I liked that. And then there was the whole thing about Christmas Eve and the anniversary of the accident. Better to be in a place with no memories, where I could work alone all night in my studio and not have to remember.

December 2, 1972
Dear Anna,

I'm taking a photography course so I've made some cards to show you what it's like out here. This is a photo of a container ship coming into the harbour. You can see a tugboat just behind it, helping to escort it into port.

How are things in the Peg? How's school? Things here are good. I like Halifax, it reminds me a bit of Fort McKay. My house is near Citadel Hill and when you stand on the hill and look down at the harbour it's a lot like standing up on Hillcrest Park looking down at the lake.

I'm still getting used to things at school. NSCAD isn't what I expected. There's a lot of reading which is OK.

The thing I don't like are the crits—that's when you have to stand in front of the class and talk about your work and everyone critiques it, which usually means ripping it apart. I'm getting a tougher skin though, which is probably a good thing.

Sorry I won't see you at Christmas, but hope you all have a great time.

Molly

When the Christmas madness started I tried to keep a low profile. Everyone was talking about heading home and how great it was going to be to have the family all together. They'd go through all their family rituals of special foods and traditions and whether they opened their presents Christmas Eve or Christmas morning. When they asked me about my plans I just said my family didn't celebrate Christmas—that quickly put an end to the conversation.

I walked to the college on Christmas Eve and the streets were empty. It had been snowing, but the temperature rose and the snow turned to sleet and then rain.

There was no one at the college except the commissionaire. I wound my way through the old building, along a labyrinth of narrow halls and stairs that seemed to wind in all directions like an Escher print. I had a key to my studio and I turned on the light and hung up my wet coat. It was cold. They'd turned the heat down in the building for the holidays.

I put a new canvas on the easel and sat looking at it. The wind blew the rain against the window. I didn't want to be there. I didn't want to be alone at Christmas. I wanted to be home with Toivo and Kiiko, but I couldn't. If I had gone back to Fort McKay I know that on Christmas Eve I would have put on my coat and walked out the door and down the street. I would have gone around the corner and walked up to the house with the red door where I had grown up. I would have stood in front of that door and seen two cops walking up the sidewalk, and I would have seen a frightened girl open the door. And when she opened the door I would have seen her world fall apart.

March 15, 1973
Dear Kiiko and Toivo,

This is a photo of the harbour on a really cold day in February. The white mist sitting on the water is called sea smoke and the dark shadow you see coming through the sea smoke is the Dartmouth ferry.

I can't believe my first year is almost over. I did well, considering. Got a great mark in art history, which was good. And I have some news—I got a job. I'm going to be working in a small art gallery in Lunenburg for the summer. It doesn't pay a lot, but I get to live in an apartment above the gallery for free. It's good experience and will look good on my resume. Look at me, eh, talking about jobs and resumes. Anyway, sorry I won't be back for the summer. Hope everything back home is OK. I'll send you some pictures from Lunenburg when I get there.

Oh, and Happy St. Urho's Day!

Molly

I looked at the photo of the sea smoke rising in white plumes on the harbour. It obscured the view of the city and the McDonald bridge and the ships. That's what living in Halifax was like. Everything was obscured—not quite visible. I was lonely, but I didn't want to tell Toivo and Kikko. I knew they would be disappointed about my staying in Nova Scotia for the summer. They wouldn't say so, but I knew they would be. Toivo had been doing some work on my house and I know he was excited for me to see it. He told me if I wanted to put in a bigger garden he could get a friend with a tractor to work up another quarter acre. He thought squash might do well. I needed the experience in the gallery though and I was excited about living in Lunenburg. The room above the gallery had a studio space so I would be able to paint all summer. I was working on a painting of Dad out in the boat with Nakina. The paintings kept them close.

December 19, 1973
Hi Anna,

   This is a photo of the Split Crow which is a bar beside the art college where a lot of the students hang out. It's not the Wayland Hotel, but I think you'd like it.
   So your mom tells me you're getting serious about some guy from Winnipeg. Is he someone from the university? Is he doing a law degree? What's he like? I want all the details.
   Things here are OK. One of the things I was looking forward to was figure drawing, but that is considered too old school for the conceptual art folks so a bunch of students have organized an underground figure drawing class off campus.

Oh and I'm learning weaving. I know what you're thinking—me, weaving. I thought I'd be crap but turns out I love it. It takes a lot of patience, especially setting up the loom, but I love the texture of the wools and the colours. If I ever move back to the cabin in Kamanistiquia I think I'll get a loom.

You know I told you I was taking constructed forms this term—well I am going to have a piece in the NSCAD student show this spring. It's called Stone Man. I created it with eight pieces of Plexiglas which have been heated and moulded to form the outline of the Sleeping Giant.

Glad to hear you're going to be going home at Christmas, but I'm afraid I'm not going to make it. Too much work and I'm really behind in a couple of essays, so I'll stay on here.

Molly

In the spring I worked at the NSCAD gallery to assemble the installation for Stone Man. We had trouble with the lighting, which was supposed to ebb and flow like the northern lights and in the end had to get a new projector. I struggled with the artist's statement. In my first attempt I tried to put the sculpture into some context:

The Stone Man is a representation of the Sleeping Giant, a formation of mesas and sills that rise out of Lake Superior. Formed from ancient Precambrian rock, the Sleeping Giant is over 1.3 billion years old.

That sounded wrong. I wasn't doing a geology paper. I had to go beyond structure:

> The Sleeping Giant, known as Nanna Bijou by the Ojibwe people, led his people to great riches of silver, but when his people were betrayed and a white man was led to the silver, Nanna Bijou was angered and rose up in a violent rage and in his wrath brought forth a great storm. When the storm had calmed and his people came out to see what was left of their world, they found Nanna Bijou turned to stone, lying across the harbour, arms crossed—feet forever guarding the silver treasure.

That wasn't right either. The Stone Man wasn't just geology or mythology. To me he was personal:

> Geology gives him structure, mythology gives him story. He is a wonder of the world, and a wonder of my world. Always present, ever watching, ancient wisdom.

It was short and sweet and all that needed to be said.

June 24, 1974
Dear Toivo and Kiiko,

> *I took this photo from the middle of the MacDonald Bridge and you can see across the harbour out to the ocean. The lighthouse you can see is on George's Island.*
> *I can't believe I'm graduating in three weeks. I wish*

you could be here for the convocation, but I know it's hard for you to get away. Thanks so much for the box of goodies. I shared the Kivela bakery coffee bread with my roommates and they could see why I keep talking about it.

I had a talk with my academic advisor and I've decided to continue on and do my masters. He was very encouraging and it will only be another two years.

I'm putting an exhibition together as part of my application to the masters program and Dr. Thompson, my advisor, has suggested that I apply to some galleries once it's complete because it would be good to get my work seen. I'm going to apply to the gallery I worked at in Lunenburg and a couple in Toronto, and I plan to apply to the new art gallery in Fort McKay. If I get accepted then I'll have a chance to get home to see you.

I'll get my friends to take some photos of the graduation and I'll send them to you.

Oh and thanks Toivo for taking care of the house for me. It must have been a lot of work to clean out that old well. I was reading your description of scooping out the dead rats to my roommate Terry and it almost made her puke! I'm glad you took the water samples in to get tested. Let me know when you get the results back.

Miss you guys

Molly

I was nervous about the graduate student show, but in the end it all went well. There were twelve of us who submitted pieces to the show and we cheered each other on and had a great party at the Split Crow after the open-ing. The Stone Man was well received, though most peo-ple didn't really understand it. If you're from Fort McKay the Sleeping Giant is in your blood and doesn't need an explanation.

July 29, 1974
Hi Anna,

I took this photo from the top of the Dartmouth ferry at night and the lights you see are the Halifax skyscape. The moon was full that night and you can see the reflection on the water.

Well, your mom and dad told me all about your visit, and they've given Kevin the thumbs up. I'm really happy for you.

I've been working on pieces for my masters exhibition and it has been rough. I need to finish it in a month, so I'm pulling a lot of all-nighters. Did I tell you about the show? I'm using the paintings I did back when I was working in that crazy little studio on the top of the Sask Pool.

I have three paintings of Nakina in the show. Do you remember that time she was in the powwow up on the mountain? She was wearing the jingle dress she got from Rocky Lake, and Dad took a picture of her. Well, I've been working on that painting for about a week or more. We're standing side by side and I have my arm over her shoulder and Nakina's got this silly grin on her face and she's got her two fingers sticking up like feathers at the back of my head. What a goofball.

I wish I knew where she was, Anna. I just want to know she's OK. If you hear anything about her, I know, you're in the Peg, but if you hear anything let me know, OK?

Molly

By the end of August I had all the pieces ready for the exhibit. The artist's statement was written. As I waited for Dr. Thompson to arrive I read it over one more time.

Witness

In 1968, with a Brownie Camera and black and white film, I went out into the streets of my hometown, Fort McKay, Ontario. I was a shy kid who melted invisibly into the background, and that day I realized invisibility gave me a unique perspective. I walked unseen through the day, my camera a dispassionate observer. I stopped time, and in that suspended plane I saw beauty in the small details that connected the people and place.

The paintings are done in black and white and I have used colour to lead the eye into the heart of the image. In these simple images can be found a layered and complex portrait of the human politics of a small northern town.

Here is a town suspended in a moment before change—before the closing of the grain elevators and the shutting down of the mill. This is the moment before the shops and movie theatres become boarded up because so many were out of work.

Look beneath these details to see the narrative below. Witness the wealthy ladies in their fur coats and the white men in black suits who run the town. Look at the grain handlers and millworks who crossed the ocean to find a better life. Look at men sleeping rough on park benches and native children held captive behind the chain link fence of the residential school.

The hands of the clock on the tower have stopped and in that suspended animation we can see all the layers that connect. We see the fierce frontier spirit and below it a dark layer of racism and class division. Look deeper at the strata below and see a pristine land before Europeans, before the fur trade. Look at the pines twisted in the wind and the silver hidden safe below the Stone Man.

Witness it all, good and bad, set in stark isolation on a rugged geography, the people as strong and resilient as the granite shield below.

"You've been busy."

I hadn't noticed Dr. Thompson come into my studio. "I've added four new pieces." I said.

He took the artist's statement from my hand and walked around the room slowly. I could feel the muscles in my gut clench. He was tough on students and didn't hold back with his opinions. I admired that—in theory. Not as easy to take when I was on the firing line. I watched his face to see if I could read his reaction. Nothing.

After walking around the room he dropped down in a chair across from me and read the papers I'd put in his hands. Every so often he would look up and look around the room at the images. Felt like I was sitting there for hours.

Finally Dr. Thompson raised his head and said, "So what?"

I looked confused.

"What's it about?" He said gesturing to the paintings.

"Well, I thought I explained in my artist's statement why…"

He lowered his glasses on his nose, raised the paper and read, "To witness the people and place. "

"Yes." I said.

"You 'suspended time.' Big deal. What you don't say is why. Why that time and that place?"

"I don't understand."

"Almost all the work you've done over the past three years is linked to that time and place. Why?"

"I don't know."

"You need to know. If you can't answer that question then all this means nothing."

I got up and walked around the room. The basket man,

Mary Christmas, the clock tower, Dad in the boat with the Stone Man behind him.

I looked at the photos mounted beside each painting, yellowing with age, edges torn. The photos were just the outside shell of what I was trying to say. But what was I trying to say?

I looked at the painting of the oak tree in front of Knox United Church and the painting of Nakina in the jingle dress. Nakina sitting in the booth at the Lorna Doone. Me with my camera reflected in the window taking the shot of Nakina in the restaurant.

The paintings were a way to hold on to Nakina when she had been gone so long. They got under the skin of the photos to the emotional places where words could not go. So much left unsaid.

I turned to Dr. Thompson, certain now.

"I'm sorry." I said.

"What for?"

"You asked me why I keep going back to that place and time. I keep going back because I need to say what I didn't say then. I'm sorry."

"Then say it." He got up and walked out of the room.

I picked up the painting of Nakina and put it on the easel and with a fine tipped brush began to paint each word on the glass of the window of the Lorna Doone.

"I watched them hurt you and did nothing. I'm sorry."

The Lunenburg gallery politely declined. Well, I understood—they were a small gallery and were already booked for over a year. The gallery in Toronto was encouraging, but they also declined. When the letter arrived from the Fort McKay Gallery I wasn't hopeful.

Dear Ms. Bell,

We have reviewed your proposal and are pleased to inform you that we would like to host your show "Witness" at the Fort McKay Art Gallery.

Given the subject matter of your show and the fact that you are from Fort McKay we feel it is an excellent fit with our mandate to support new and emerging northern artists.

We have an opening in the new year, and as we are preparing our promotional material now I would need you to confirm with us as soon as possible. Once we receive your confirmation we can discuss details. Sincerely,

Merika Goodchild

I sat holding the letter for a long time. I read it over and over again. I had a show. In Fort McKay. It was what I wanted, what I had worked for, and yet…holding the letter in my hand made it real, which meant that the work that had been private for so long would be public, and the idea of feeling so exposed terrified me. People might hate it. People in Fort McKay might be offended by what I had to say, and what if the show wasn't good enough?

I packed a sleeping bag and some food in a backpack and took the letter with me. I rented a car and drove down the coast to a provincial park and hiked in for half a day, finally setting up camp by a small lake. I needed to get away and I needed to be in the bush. That night I cooked a pot of beans over the fire and sat by the edge of the lake looking at the reflection of the moon in the water. It felt good to be out of the city. In the silence of the woods I thought about the offer from the gallery. I could say no to the exhibit. I could. Wait till I felt ready—more confident about my work. But when would that be? No, I had been working for years towards this moment. I had an exhibit. In Fort McKay. I wasn't going to run away.

When I got back to Halifax I wrote a letter accepting the offer and phoned Toivo and Kikko. Kikko was over the moon, and Toivo said he was really proud of me, which choked me up so I had to tell him I had a cold and that was why my voice sounded weird.

———◇———

That spring, the night before the opening, I walked down Main Street for the first time in many years. The stores were closed. Some men were hanging around on the street waiting for Mission House to open, all their worldly belongings tucked under their arms. Beside the shelter the windows of the Lorna Doone restaurant were boarded up with plywood. In the apartment above the restaurant a pigeon perched on the cracked glass of a window. It was serenading the homeless men with its coos. The hardware store was gone, replaced by a government office, and the hotel on the corner was now an apartment building. My footsteps echoed as I walked, and there was a sense of melancholy in the street.

I got back into Toivo's truck and drove down to the waterfront. As I walked out onto the wharf, the sun was setting behind the reclining figure of the Stone Man. I sat down on the edge of the wharf, swinging my legs over the side the way I used to when I was a kid, waiting for Dad to bring the boat around. I looked out at my old friend, the Stone Man. *Always present, ever watching, ancient wisdom.* He had been waiting patiently for me to come home.

The night of the opening Kikko and Toivo walked into the gallery beside me. The lobby was crowded. People were standing around drinking wine and a young man was circulating with a tray of hors d'oeuvres. Beyond the lobby I could see people walking around the exhibit hall. Someone offered me some food but I was too nervous to eat.

I saw people standing in front of my paintings. I saw faces I recognized from school, from the library, friends of my parents. Here to see my work. I felt naked.

I hadn't felt this way at the graduate student show. It was different in Halifax—no one knew me and I wasn't exhibiting alone. Coming back to Fort McKay brought all my old insecurities to the surface. Standing there that night I was still the weird, skinny, silent kid who never fit in.

"Molly, good, you're here." Merika Goodchild grabbed me by the arm and steered me forward through the crowd into the main exhibition hall and introduced me to a photographer from the local newspaper. He took a photo of me in front of the painting of Nakina at the Doone, which was hung in the centre of the hall. He asked a few questions about the paintings but it was hard to concentrate with all the people milling around.

The room was getting crowded and I couldn't find Kikko

or Toivo. I needed to get some air so I made my way out of the main exhibition hall into a side gallery and sat down on a bench.

"I thought I'd find you here."

I looked up to see Merika smiling at me. She handed me a glass of water.

"So?" I asked.

"Relax Molly. People love it. It's a great show."

"The lighting on the Stone Man looks good." I said.

"It does. I wanted to tell you that I think the painting of the residential school being torn down is really powerful."

"Thanks."

"My grandmother was at that residential school. She never said much but I know it was hard for her there. She was happy the day it was torn down. A lot of people were. Did you know Morriseau was there?"

"Norval Morriseau?"

She nodded to the paintings around the room. "Founder of the Woodland School. One of Canada's greatest artists. He was at the residential school."

"I didn't know that."

"He was there for a short time, then he went back up north to live with his grandfather, who was a shaman, and began painting. These two panels," she pointed directly across from where we were sitting, "form a diptych titled 'The Storyteller,' painted in honour of his grandfather Moses Nanakonagos."

I looked at the two tall narrow panels. In the panel on the left, in deep blues and strong reds, was the powerful presence of the shaman storyteller. The panel to the right was more muted with yellows and browns and the small figure of a boy looking upward, receiving wisdom. Between them birds swirled in black-lined circles of deeper and deeper blue, eyes yellow, piercing the soul.

"We should go back in," Merika said. "Time to get the formal part of the evening out of the way. You OK now?"

"I'm good."

I went back into the main hall with Merika and she gathered people around the middle of the room.

"Good evening everyone. My name is Merika Goodchild and I am the Director of the Fort McKay Art Gallery. I want to welcome you here tonight to the launch of our inaugural series of new and emerging northern artists. This series is designed to nurture artists whose artistic vision has its roots in the north. It is my great pleasure to introduce Molly Bell, who tonight launches her show 'Witness.' In a series of acrylic images Ms. Bell suspends a moment in time in Fort McKay in 1968. In describing her work, Molly Bell says, 'In these images can be found the layered and complex portrait of the human politics of a small northern town.' Please welcome Molly Bell."

I stepped to the front of the crowd and could feel my legs shaking. I had prepared some notes to introduce the show but as I looked over at Toivo's smiling face I slipped the notes into my pocket. "It is good to be home," I said. "When my plane was landing the other day we flew over the Nor'Westers and across the Kam River over the Riverview Cemetery. In that cemetery, buried in the red clay soil along the banks of the Kam, lie my ancestors—my parents, grandparents and great grandparents. My roots are here. I grew up in the shadow of the Stone Man. This is the geography that shaped me and the inspiration for 'Witness.' It is an honour to be here tonight to share my work with you. Thank you."

When the crowd began to thin Kikko and Toivo grabbed Merika and asked her to take a photo of the three of us in front of the Stone Man. Toivo was complaining that there wasn't any beer and Kikko said her feet were killing her so I headed to the lobby to get our coats. I walked across the exhibition hall. As I passed the centre of the hall I noticed a woman in a red dress.

She was tall, with dark skin, and her hair was pulled up under a silk scarf. She was looking at the painting of Nakina—Nakina sitting at the Lorna Doone—me outside the restaurant reflected in the glass. The words of silent apology between us. As I walked behind her, the woman in the red dress turned.

Nakina.

For a moment we stood frozen, and as I moved toward her the space between us dissolved. I held her tight, afraid to break the embrace. Afraid that if I let go she would dissolve in my arms. We stood together locked tight and I felt the sharpness of her ribs and the bones of her shoulder blades. Too thin. I pulled back to look at her face. Thin, drawn but beautiful.

"Hey white girl," she said.

"Hey Anishinaabe. I can't believe you're here."

"I told you I'd come to your show when it opened. Remember?"

"Yeah. I remember, but I never thought you'd…"

"You changed the name of the show. 'Witness,' very artsy. Personally I thought 'Piss Off' was a better title."

"Very funny," I said.

"You haven't changed. Still a bean pole."

"Of course. You look good."

"Bullshit." Nakina put her hand to the edge of the scarf and pushed it back a few inches. Underneath her head was bare except for a few soft hairs.

"Oh god, Nakina. "

"It's not as bad as it looks."

"Cancer?"

"Breast cancer. But I've finished three rounds of chemo and I'm feeling great."

Merika interrupted. "Molly, can I grab you before you leave?"

"Sure. Just give me a few minutes." I turned back to Nakina. "Where are you living?"

"I have an apartment near the hospital."

"Can we get together tomorrow? God, I still can't believe it."

"I have an appointment at the hospital tomorrow at ten. We can get together after that."

"Why don't I meet you at the hospital. I have Toivo's truck. There's someplace I want to take you."

chapter twenty-three

Nakina slept the whole drive to Kamanistiquia. I rolled up my coat for a pillow and she curled up on the seat and went to sleep. The appointment at the hospital had not gone well. When I got there she was still in the waiting room. I thought she might have someone with her, but she was alone. I sat down.

"Have you been waiting long?" I asked.

"About fifteen minutes."

I looked at her and saw the worry in her face.

"Are you OK?" I asked.

"What do you think?" she smiled at me.

"Do you want mc to go in with you?"

"Would you?"

"Of course."

When Nakina was called we went into a small examination cubicle. There were only two seats so I stood. The doctor didn't waste any time with small chat.

"We have the results of your tests, and they're not what

we had hoped to see. The tumour has continued to grow despite the treatments, and the CT scan shows evidence of metastases in your liver and lungs."

"So, what does that mean? What happens next?" Nakina asked.

"We've exhausted our options I'm afraid."

"There must be something."

"We'll keep you comfortable."

I looked across at Nakina but her face was stiff.

"How long?" she asked.

"We can't really say. Every patient is…"

"How long? Best guess," she said.

With no emotion in his voice he said, "You need to think of your life now in terms of months, not years." He asked if we had any further questions. Nakina said nothing, just got up and left the room.

She didn't speak again until we got back to the truck. "I feel nauseous."

"Should I take you back to your apartment?" I asked.

"No. I'll be OK. I just need to lie down."

Nakina was still asleep when I pulled the truck into the driveway of my house in Kamanistiquia. I didn't want to wake her so I slipped quietly out of the truck and walked past the house into the field in front of the barn. I had been away a long time. I closed my eyes and drank in the smell of pine and cedar. I turned and looked at the house. Still standing solid. I looked up at the hills and remembered the ski trails I'd made back in the woods. When I turned again I saw Nakina sitting up. I walked back to the truck.

"How are you feeling?" I asked.

"Where are we?" She got out, stretched and looked around.

"Kamanistiquia. My place. I lived here for a year before I went east. Come on inside, I'll put a fire on."

"You go ahead. I need some time alone." Her voice was flat.

"Sure."

Nakina walked past the house into the field. I got out the key and opened the door. The house smelled musty. Standing at the kitchen window I saw Nakina walking slowly across the field. I could see the anger in her body as she walked. She stopped outside the barn, picked up some broken bricks and went around the side of the barn, out of sight. Silence and then a wailing, raging scream and the sound of shattered glass as the bricks hit the barn windows.

I couldn't move. After a time the screaming stopped and there was silence. I waited. There was nothing I could do.

When I went to her she was sitting in the grass. I sat beside her and put my arm around her. It was early spring and the ground was still cold. In the sky a formation of geese was returning home.

We went inside and she sat by the stove. I boiled some water and found a tin with tea bags in the cupboard. We didn't say much. I knew she needed to think.

"Is this yours?" She was looking at Celeste's painting.

"No, a friend of mine painted that. Really sweet kid."

"So you really lived here?"

"I did."

"Alone?"

"Yes."

Nakina got up and walked through the kitchen into the living room. She stood cupping her mug of tea and looked out the window. "Months, not years," she said. "I thought…I felt like I was getting better. I thought the news would be good."

When I got back to town I told Kikko and Toivo what was happening and asked them if I could stay with them a while. Kikko told me I didn't have to ask.

I phoned Halifax and let the college know I wouldn't be back for a few months.

Toivo told me there was a message for me from Merika. She'd sold two paintings, the basket man and Mary Christmas. The guy who bought Mary Christmas said he knew me and left his phone number. I looked at the piece of paper Toivo handed me. Lars. I put the number in my wallet.

The next day I went to Nakina's apartment. She offered me coffee and we spent some time looking at old photographs. She still had the shoebox full of photos she'd taken up at Rocky Lake. "That's Auntie," she said. "She made the Jingle dress for me. And Moses."

"I remember. I still have all the letters you sent me from Rocky Lake," I said.

Nakina went to the closet and came back with the stack of letters I had sent to her that summer, tied up with a leather string. She read some of the letters and we looked at photos and laughed. She told me more about being in Rocky Lake, and it was clear that her time up north was a touchstone for everything that came after.

It was so good to be with her but the more we talked the more I could feel we were talking in circles around the things we couldn't say, the weight of those things pushing us apart.

Over the next few weeks I drove Nakina to the hospital for tests and appointments. Kikko made homemade soup, but Nakina wasn't very hungry. We still didn't say much. She was getting weaker so I focused on helping her feel comfortable. After a month a bed was available on the palliative care floor and Nakina was admitted. I knew she didn't want to go, but she was so weak she could hardly get up to go to the bathroom.

The day I took her to the hospital she packed a small bag. "Is that all you're taking?" I said.

"I have a favour to ask."

"Sure."

"Here's the keys to the apartment. After you drop me off could you come back and sort out the last things. I've left a note on the table telling you what you need to do. Then drop the keys with the landlady downstairs."

"No problem. Don't worry about it."

"Thanks."

"Nakina?"

"Yeah."

"Do you think maybe sometime we could talk?"

She looked up at me and I knew she understood what I was saying, but she brushed it off. "What do you think we've been doing?"

"I know, it's just…there are some things I'd like to talk about."

Nakina looked so weary I didn't push it any further.

I left Nakina in the admitting department at the hospital and told her I would come back that afternoon once she was settled into her room. I went back to her apartment and found the note on the table. She had left a list of things she needed me to do: 1) clean out the fridge, 2) take out the garbage, 3) there's some canned food in the cupboard, take it if you want it, 4) all the towels and linens stay, 5) there is a suitcase of clothes in the closet you can do whatever you want with, and a box of photos and stuff I thought you might like, 6) on the table is a file with some papers including a copy of my will. Take it to Mitch. He is expecting it.

It didn't take me long to clean out the apartment. I loaded the suitcase and box into the truck and took the file to the Native Friendship Centre. It was good to see Mitch again after so many years. He told me Nakina was leaving her money to the Friendship Centre to go into a fund they were raising to build a childcare centre.

I headed back to the hospital in the afternoon. The palliative care wing was on the seventh floor. When I got off the elevator I saw a stained glass mandala called the tree of life—the moon was its roots and the sun its branches. I could see angels everywhere. Angel mobiles hanging over the desk, angel photos on the walls, angel figurines on the desk. Gifts from families I guessed. Seemed creepy though.

I didn't think people needed wall-to-wall angels to remind them that everyone there was dying.

Behind the nursing station was a large whiteboard with the names of the patients, their room numbers and the nurse assigned to them that day. Nakina Wabasoon, room 734—Hodder.

I walked past the nursing station, past a room with a sign that read "kitchenette." Looked like a place where people could make a cup of tea or some toast. Beside the kitchenette was a room set up to look all cozy and homey with a fake fireplace and blaring television that no one was watching. There was a half-finished jigsaw puzzle on a card table.

Room 734 was at the end of the corridor, so I had to run the gauntlet of dozens of rooms to get to it. I looked straight ahead because I didn't want to see what was going on in those other rooms.

When I got to Nakina's room she was asleep. I slipped into the chair beside her bed and waited. She looked small –a bald, shrivelled-up Nakina. She had an IV line in her arm, and her johnny shirt covered only one shoulder. I felt like pulling the blanket up over her bare shoulder but I didn't want to wake her.

I felt awkward about watching her. Her face looked older. She used to have such great cheekbones, but her face looked puffy and there were dark circles under her eyes. I was still trying to get used to the bald head. I tried imagining her with her long black hair and put my hand up over my eyes to see if I could pretend she had bangs.

"Playing peek-a-boo?"

"Hey Anishinaabe," I said.

"Hey white girl."

"How are you feeling?"

"Crap."

"Nice room," I said. "You can see the Sleeping Giant from your window."

"Good, a room with a view. Did you get that stuff to Mitch?"

"I did."

"Thanks." She closed her eyes and I thought she was drifting off to sleep again but she mumbled, "I was in the Psychiatric Hospital."

"What?"

"The Lakehead Psychiatric Hospital—the LPH."

"The nuthouse?"

"Yeah."

"When?"

Nakina didn't answer; she was asleep.

That night at dinner I told Kikko what Nakina had said.

"The psychiatric hospital? Oh yeah, that's right. She was there."

"When?"

"Back in high school," Kikko said.

"Why?"

"It's where they sent her when she got pregnant."

"You knew about that?"

"Of course. Everybody did."

"I don't get it. Why did they send her to a psychiatric hospital to have a baby?"

"That's where they sent the Indian girls who got pregnant."

"So, she was right here in town. All those months she was away from school she was just a few miles away."

"That's right."

We sat down at the table and I filled my plate with Finnish pancakes and sausages. I was thinking about Nakina in the psychiatric hospital—thinking about what happened that put her there. I looked up at Kikko.

"What?" she asked.

I started to speak, but the words wouldn't come out. I put my head down, took a deep breath and tried again. "I was there that day." I said.

"What day?"

"The day Nakina was attacked."

"Attacked?"

I looked at Toivo and Kikko, and after so many years of silence the words finally came.

"Not attacked," I said. "Raped. She was raped by Bernie Olfson, the cop."

"Olfson. Christ Molly, are you sure?" Toivo asked.

"I saw it."

"What do you mean?"

"She had an epilepsy attack, beside the Lorna Doone. At least I think that's how she ended up on the ground. I don't know. I was waiting for her in the restaurant and she didn't come. She said she'd be right in so I went outside to see where she was, and there were these cops back in the alley and they had her on the ground and Bernie Olfson was on her."

"Son of a bitch!" said Toivo.

"It happened a lot then," Kiiko said.

"Cops raping young girls?" I asked.

"Cops raping Indian girls," Toivo said.

"And they got away with it?"

"Yeah, well what were the kids going to do, call the cops?"

chapter twenty-four

The next day Nakina was awake when I walked in. She looked up at me. "You look like shit,"

"Not much sleep," I said. "How do you feel today?"

"When the morphine goes in, good. When it's gone, bad."

"And now?"

"Bad."

Nakina closed her eyes and I sat down and waited. I wasn't sure if she was asleep. With eyes still closed she said, "You wanted to talk?"

"What?"

"Yesterday when we were leaving my apartment. You said you wanted to talk."

"Yeah, but not today." I could see the pain in her face. "You don't feel well today."

"I feel like crap every day. I'm dying. If you have something to say, say it."

"No Nakina, this isn't a good…"

"Stop!"

"Stop what?" I asked, surprised at the anger in her voice.

"Stop being so fucking polite."

I turned away from her and looked out the window. Heavy slate-grey clouds were coming in from the west. They parted for a moment and the sun broke through, sending a long band of light across the crossed arms of the Stone Man.

"I'm not being polite."

Nakina opened her eyes. "Nice polite little white girl wouldn't say shit if your mouth was full of it. That always pissed me off about you."

"I'll get the nurse."

"No. We're going to talk. What did you want to say?"

I got up and looked out the window again. I could see a ship on the horizon. Coming in from Toronto maybe. I turned to face Nakina. So much I needed to understand.

"Where did you go?" I asked.

"When?"

"That night after I saw you on Simpson Street."

"I left town."

"Why?"

"It wasn't safe. I wasn't safe."

I turned to look out the window again. I was back on Simpson Street on that frigid winter night, painting under my arm looking at a hooker standing at the curb, rocking back and forth on her stiletto-heeled boots. And then she turned and flicked her long black hair away from her face. Nakina. Nakina in a fur coat looking down the street at the cars. Looking for her next john and instead she saw me.

"You kept disappearing," I said. "That day in high school

you cleaned out your locker and left. You never talked to me, never told me what happened."

"What could I say? I couldn't tell you.'

"You could have."

"You had no goddamed clue Molly. No goddamed clue what my life was like. What did you want me to tell you? That the school janitor was screwing me? That his wife set it all up—took in native foster kids for her husband to screw? Is that what you wanted me to tell you?"

"Nakina. I didn't know."

"How could you? I couldn't talk to you. Not about that stuff."

I turned to look out the window again. The rain had started.

"So that's why you left high school?"

"I went to Social Services and told them what was going on."

"What happened?"

"They investigated and he denied everything. Of course. He was so pissed off with me for reporting him that he took that money from the school office and hid it in my room. The next day when the school realized the money was missing, he told them he'd seen me hide it in my room. The principal called the cops and they searched my room and found the money. My word against his. They kicked me out of school."

I could see beads of sweat across Nakina's forehead and I got a cold cloth and wiped her face. Her hands were clenched tight with pain.

"Let me get some help. I'll call the nurse."

"No. I need to tell you. I got kicked out of school. I

didn't have any place to live." Nakina stopped for a few minutes. "I had a friend. From the residential school. She was working on Simpson Street. I moved into the hotel with her. She introduced me to the guy she worked for."

"Her pimp?"

"He talked me into working for him. Said if I was going to get screwed by white guys I might as well get paid. I thought maybe he was right. Maybe it was a better option. I didn't have a lot of choices."

"That's how you ended up working on the street."

"That night on the street. When I turned around. You saw me and you turned away."

"I didn't…I didn't expect…"

"Why were you even there that night Molly? Why were you walking down Simpson Street?'

"I was looking for you."

"Well you found me."

We looked at each other for a few moments.

"After you walked away a car pulled over and I got in," she said. "Told the guy to take me to North Fort, to the Friendship Centre."

"Why?"

"Because I thought of another option."

"So you went to Mitch?"

"I was lucky. The guy who picked me up took me to the Friendship Centre and Mitch was there. I told him everything. He took me home and his wife Marcia called her sister in Sault Ste. Marie. They said I had to get out of Fort McKay fast. It wasn't safe to stay. They'd be looking for me. Marcia's sister let me stay with her in the Sault while I took some courses at the college there. Mitch arranged it all."

"So that's where you've been. In Sault Ste. Marie?"

"For a while. I trained to be a court reporter, and when I graduated I got a job with the government working out west on native land claims hearings. That's what I've been doing. Travelling a lot. Mostly in British Columbia. I came back here when I got sick."

"So, you were on one edge of the country and I was on the other."

"Molly?"

"Yes."

"Can you get the nurse now?"

I pressed the call button and as we waited for the nurse to come Nakina turned to me. "I had to go right away. I didn't have a choice."

"I know."

"It was that night wasn't it—the night I saw you on the street?"

"What was?"

"The accident. Your mom and dad. Mitch told me. But I had to go."

"It's OK." I rubbed her shoulder and could feel her body shaking. "It's OK."

They increased the dose of morphine and Nakina slept for the rest of the day. I left the hospital early and drove down to the waterfront. I walked along the wharf beside the grain elevators. I thought about Mom and Dad and how much I missed them every single day.

I thought about the funeral and how softly and silently the snow had fallen on the steeple of the church. How it fell in a soft blanket onto the street making the world silent and still. I thought about how, on that day, as I followed my parents' coffins down the steps of the church, Nakina was flying away. Flying to safety.

———◇———

"What's that?" Nakina opened her eyes and tried to focus on what I had put on the tray in front of her.

"It's a cribbage board."

"What for?"

"What do you think? To play cribbage."

"You hate cribbage," she said.

"I know, but you don't."

"Can you get me a glass of water first?"

I poured Nakina a glass of ice water and held the straw to her lips. "OK?"

"Thanks."

"I'll deal." I laid down six cards each and Nakina cut the deck. I turned up the top card.

"Jack—dealer pegs two," I said, moving my marker along the board.

"I didn't even know you knew how to play. You always had your head in a book when your mom and dad and I were playing."

"I read a book on how to play."

"Very funny. Why didn't you want to play with us?" she asked.

"I liked lying on the couch reading and listening to you guys talk. Very entertaining. Every time mom said 'and one for his knobs' I'd crack up."

"That was pretty funny."

"Fifteen two, fifteen four." Nakina lifted her hand out

from under the blanket and moved her pin along the board.

"Run." I moved four spaces along the board. We played for about an hour until the nurse came in to change the IV bag. I helped her shift Nakina into a new position to keep the pressure off her hips. I had bought some special Moroccan oil that was supposed to be good for bedsores and massaged it into her shoulders and arms. Then I helped her sit up while I changed her Johnny shirt. I could see she was exhausted. She fell asleep as soon as she lay back on her pillow.

While she slept I went across the street to George's diner for lunch. Sitting at the booth I started to draw up some plans for the garden. I could dig up another quarter acre and put in squash, like Toivo suggested. And I was thinking of adding a porch to the house along the south side. It would be nice in winter to capture as much sun as possible.

Once I decided to move back out to the house I talked to Toivo. "I need a car," I said.

"No."

"I do. I want to move out to the…"

"No, you don't need a car. You need a truck."

"Oh."

"A good truck that will handle those back roads even in the middle of winter. I got one picked out for you."

"Oh yeah, some broken-down piece of crap one of your friends at the Wayland is trying to get rid of?"

"Very funny. No. I'll take you tomorrow."

Toivo drove me into town the next day and we pulled into the lot of Lakehead Auto. A guy came out as soon as he saw us and showed us a few trucks. Toivo had his eye on a brand new red Ford pick-up.

"So you had this all worked out?" I said.

"Knew you'd need a truck to get back and forth."

"And you knew I was going to stay?"

"Of course."

I paid cash that afternoon and drove the truck off the lot. Toivo took a photo of me in front of the truck and said he was going to send it to Anna.

I packed my stuff, loaded up the truck and stopped at the mall on the way out of town to stock up on supplies—food, linens, two new Coleman lamps and lamp oil. I stopped at the farm supply store and picked up two twenty-pound bags of seed potatoes and a new spade and hoe. I got some seeds too—kale, squash, carrots, zucchini, beets. They grew well in the red clay soil. The sun was starting to set when I got to the house.

I lit a fire in the stove and went into the bedroom. My overalls were still hanging from a hook on the wall. It seemed strange, like I'd never been away. I stripped the bed and made it up with the new sheets and pillows, went back into the kitchen and unpacked the groceries. I made a pot of tea, warmed up the soup Kiiko had made and ate it with bread from the Kivela bakery. Looking out the window I traced the ragged tops of the pine trees along the edge of the road. Two blue jays squawked from the birch tree beside the well. I unpacked my suitcase and put the small black shoe from the residential school on the kitchen mantel.

When it was dark I went out behind the house and stood

in the field. The sky was clear and I could see the Milky Way and Cassiopeia. There was a thin slice of moon over the hills. Later that night I was serenaded to sleep by a chorus of wolves up in the hills.

Home.

The next day I went out to the field with the spade over my shoulder. The morning dew made the tall grass sparkle. The garden I'd dug up a few years before had not completely grown over. I put the spade on the ground, put my foot on the rim and leaned forward using my weight to drive the spade through the hard clay. I pulled back on the handle and lifted a lump of soil, turned it over and moved along the row. It felt good to be doing something physical.

I thought about Nakina as I worked. The things she had told me. About getting kicked out of school. About moving into the hotel on Simpson Street. There was no one there to protect her. No safe place.

I drove into town about noon and Nakina was asleep. Her nurse said she had been asleep all morning. They had her on a new drug.

I sat and looked out the window. I was surprised that I was missing Halifax. I missed my friends. I missed working in my studio. I missed painting.

When I had been working in the field that morning I'd looked back at the barn and thought maybe I could do something with it. It needed a new roof, but the beams inside were strong. The windows needed to be replaced, and I could knock in some extra ones along the back to get the afternoon light. It would take a bit of work but it could make a good studio. And there was lots of space to set up a loom. I was even thinking maybe I could get some sheep.

Nakina was tossing and turning and she started to mumble. I didn't know if she was awake or dreaming. It was getting harder to tell. Sometimes when I was talking to her a veil would seem to drop between us.

"I was on the train," she said.

"What train?"

"Momma put me on the train. I can't see out the window. I can't see my mother." Nakina opened her eyes and tried to sit up.

"What train were you on?" I asked.

"Can you get me some water? My mouth is dry."

I got a glass of water and held the straw to her lips. She put her head back on the pillow and I thought she would go back to sleep, but she turned to me and I could tell from the look in her eyes that her mind was clear.

"They took me to the psychiatric hospital, you know."

"You told me. To have the baby."

"There was no baby. I was just over four months. They gave me a general anesthetic and when I woke up the nurse said they'd taken care of it."

"Aborted?"

"And when they had me under the anesthetic they tied my tubes."

"I don't understand."

"Sterilized me. What they did to Indian girls who got pregnant."

"But they couldn't. They couldn't just do that."

"They could. They did. After that I got an infection and had to stay there for months."

After a while she drifted off to sleep again. Curled up in the fetal position with her bald head and so thin I could see her shoulder blades through her skin, Nakina looked like a baby bird that had fallen out of the nest.

I was holding back tears because I didn't want to cry. Didn't want to wake Nakina. Didn't want the nurses or some stranger to come in and see me crying. I thought about the day that Nakina came back to school. After what she had gone through—what they had done to her—she just came back to school and picked up her books at her locker and went off to class, like nothing had happened. What else could she do?

She slept the rest of the afternoon so I curled up in the chair and slept too. I dreamt about a train, a long black train pulled by a steam engine puffing its way through the bush. Black train, black smoke cutting a black line through the boreal forest. Past blue lakes, past moose standing up to their bony knees in the marsh, past jagged red rock cuts. Onward, farther south. Tiny faces pressed against the window. The faces of the stolen children. Nakina's face, with her mouth opened slightly as if she were about call out to someone. Call out for help.

When I woke up Nakina was still asleep. I sat in the chair in the dark room listening to the beeping sounds coming from down the hall. Every so often there would be an announcement over the hospital intercom: "Code blue, trauma team to emergency stat, trauma team to emergency." Then everything would be quiet for hours. Then there would be a flurry of activity somewhere on the floor—people running, orders shouted, someone crying. Then silence again. More waiting.

I left Nakina's room and walked down to the family room. I spent some time working on the jigsaw puzzle. I was angry but didn't know why. I think I was angry with myself. I felt so useless. The puzzle was an English thatched cottage surrounded by a rose garden. The thatched roof was a real bitch.

chapter twenty-five

The next day when I arrived at the hospital I could hear Nakina screaming all the way down the hall. I ran to her room. "Do you want me to get the nurse?" I asked. I could see she was in pain.

"I want you to get the fuck out."

She had kicked the blankets off and I could see her thin boney legs kicking against the metal rails of the bed. Nurse Hodder came in with another nurse who was carrying a tray with medication and an IV bag. I stepped back into the washroom and watched through the doorway as they worked quickly to change the line and hang the new IV bag. Nakina had stopped swearing and was making low moaning sounds. The nurses stripped the top sheets and remade the bed, swaddling her flailing arms and legs. The moans got softer till they sounded almost like a kitten purring. The nurse turned to me.

"Come here. Molly, is it?"

"Yes."

She handed me a jar of clear cream. "Could you sit there. No, pull the chair closer to the bed. Good. Now take that cream and rub it on her lips."

I was afraid to touch Nakina. Afraid she would start shouting again, afraid to feel the dry peeling skin on her lips.

But the nurse was watching. "Good. Now, try to do that every few hours. Down in the kitchenette you can get ice. Straws are in the left-hand drawer. Keep a glass of ice water by the bed. It's comforting to keep the mouth moist."

"OK."

"I went down to the kitchenette and got some large plastic glasses and straws and filled a blue water jug with ice and water. When I went back to the room Nakina was sitting up in bed."

"What the hell are you doing?" she asked.

"I brought you some ice water."

"In a urinal?"

I looked at the blue plastic water jug and realized it had an odd shaped wide spout.

"Molly, you're such an ass!" Nakina started to laugh and I dropped into the chair beside her and began to laugh hysterically. Once I got the giggles there was no going back, and the more Nakina laughed the more it set me off until a nurse stuck her head in the door.

"Everything OK?"

I held up the urinal, laughing too hard to explain. She smiled. "Yeah, you're not the first one to make that mistake. Don't know why they make them both the same colour. I'll take that."

The drugs were working. Nakina was sitting up laughing and I could tell from her face that she wasn't in pain.

We talked for more than an hour about her work in B.C. "It was interesting. Not the actual recording; that was pretty mindless. But the hearings were interesting. I learned a lot about land claim issues. A lot of legal stuff. Met some great people. Travelled a lot. Most of our work was in Northern B.C., up around Williams Lake."

"What was it like?"

"The mountains were beautiful. Snow capped. I liked hiking in the mountains. Camping out."

"Sounds good."

"It was. Until I got sick."

"And then you came back here?"

"Right. I could have gone to the hospital in Vancouver but I wanted to come back here." Nakina turned onto her back and adjusted her pillow. She looked tired. "So what about you? How is Halifax? How is the art college?"

"Good. Different from high school—I finally feel like I fit in. And there's interesting stuff going on."

"What stuff?"

"Conceptual art—more concept than form. Hard to explain. Anyway I like the East Coast. I like living beside the ocean. It reminds me of Lake Superior."

"I remember…" Nakina paused. She was drifting off again. "I remember in high school you said you were going to go to art school."

"Yeah, and you said I was an asshole and would never get out of Fort McKay."

"Guess I was wrong."

The hospital intercom came on. "Code blue 7B stat, code blue 7B stat." Two nurses ran down the corridor and into the room across from Nakina's. There was a brief flurry of activity as an oxygen cart was wheeled into the room, then everything went quiet. When I looked back over at Nakina she was asleep.

I sat quietly beside her looking at her sleeping face and thought about her hiking in the mountains. I spent the afternoon waiting. Waiting and thinking. Wondering what the end would be like. Afraid but not certain what I was afraid of.

I got up and walked around the room. Not much to see—a bed, a side table with a box of Kleenex and the jar of clear cream. In the bathroom was a toilet with metal handrails, two boxes of rubber gloves, a metal bedpan and a box labelled "Toothettes." I opened the box and pulled out a stick with a foam tip and wondered what they were for.

I looked out the window, out across the harbour. I could see a boat on the horizon. Looked like a grain boat. I wondered if grain was starting to come through the port again.

I walked down to the family room and spent some time adding pieces to the puzzle. There was a phone there. I dug in my wallet and pulled out the slip of paper with a telephone number and called Lars. It rang three times and went to voice mail. "You have reached Lars Gustoffson, Quetico Park Resource Manager…"

"Lars," I said. "This is Molly Bell. I got the message from Merika Goodchild that you bought one of the paintings, and I just wanted to call and say thanks." I paused for a moment then added, "I'm going to be in town for a while. I don't know how often you get into Fort McKay, but if you're around you can usually catch me at George's at lunchtime. You know, the diner across from the hospital. Anyway, it would be great to see you."

I didn't recognize Lars at first when he came into George's Diner. His long blond hair was cut short and his beard was gone. He still wore the round wire-rimmed glasses but he was taller than I remembered.

"Molly?"

"Lars." I stood up to shake his hand and almost knocked my knife onto the floor. He ignored my hand and embraced me.

"So, you got my message?" I said, sitting down.

"I did. I'm glad you called."

"Almost didn't recognize you with the short hair."

"You look the same. Almost the same. Your hair isn't as curly."

"Longer." I wore my hair long now, pulled back in one thick braid.

"So you're working up in Quetico Park?" I said.

"Yeah. I've been there a few years now."

"Do you like it?"

"I do. The people I work with are great and I get to work outside."

"What about music? Do you still play?"

"A bit. Not seriously. My brother and I have a band and we play a few gigs here and there."

"How's your dad? The last time we…well, your dad had broken his arm."

"Oh right, he's fine. I had to stay in Nipigon for a while to help out. I came back after the fire."

The fire. I hadn't spoken with anyone about it for years

but sitting with Lars it suddenly felt very raw. "It still feels like a dream to me, like it never happened."

"I didn't make it back for the funeral," he said.

"The coffins were so tiny. When they carried the coffins out they played Bob Dylan's 'Forever Young' and I thought how Celeste and Blue would always be young and innocent and perfect…forever."

"I was at Cripple Creek the night that Blue was born," Lars said. "Celeste was about three I think. She was an old soul, even then."

"She really was."

"I came back the week after to play at the benefit dance. When I got back I drove out to Cripple Creek Farm. I had to see it."

"Was anything left?"

"No, burned to the ground. Nothing but a field of snow. And then I went to your place."

I was confused. "But I never saw you."

"When I got there some guy came out of the house."

"Sid."

"Not very friendly. Said you didn't want to see anyone. I told him about the benefit dance the next night and I asked him to let you know."

"He didn't tell me."

"Anyway, after the benefit I went back to Nipigon."

"I'm sorry. I wish he had told me. I wish I'd known. You know, no one really told me what happened that night."

"There was nothing anyone could do. It was a chimney fire and once the roof caught, the top floor went so fast no one could get upstairs to them."

"I was pretty messed up after the fire. I slept a lot. Sid was there then. He drove me home after the funeral and stayed on at the house for a while. He wasn't there long. Then I moved to Halifax to go to college. I heard that Rita moved back to the States with her parents."

"That's right. Mary moved up north with Tom for a about a year. Last I heard they'd split up and Mary had gone back home.

"I think I want to go to Cripple Creek someday. Maybe if I could see it…it still feels like a dream."

"I'll take you some time if you want."

"Thanks."

"You said you were going to be in town for a while."

"My friend is in hospital. Cancer. They've stopped treatments. She's in palliative care."

"I'm really sorry. Listen, I'm in town most weekends…I'd like to help if I could. Maybe sit with you at the hospital if you like."

"That's very kind. Thanks. By the way, I moved back out to Kamanistiquia."

"Really?"

"Just for the summer. I'm planning to go back to Halifax in the fall to finish my degree. Hey, here is Kikko and Toivo's number. I stay at their house a lot. Give me a call next time you're in town. Maybe you could come over to their house for dinner some night. I'd like you to meet them."

The next day Nakina was awake most of the morning, but she seemed far away and didn't want to talk. I was getting bored sitting there so when the nurse came I helped her get Nakina into the wheelchair, then we stripped the bed. She taught me how to fold a sheet in half and lay it across the middle of the bottom sheet and tuck it in at the sides. Transfer sheet she called it, so that Nakina could be moved or shifted easily by people grabbing either end of the folded sheet. When the bed was made up I sprayed the sheets and pillow with a lavender spray. The nurse told me the smell of lavender was calming.

I opened the window and let the cool breeze off the lake clean the hospital stink out of the room. We moved Nakina back to the bed, took off her johnny shirt and gave her a sponge bath. I was uncomfortable at first, touching her body, seeing her small empty breasts and the loose skin across her belly, but I watched the nurse. She worked fast and was gentle like she was bathing her own child. I stopped looking at Nakina's body and began to think of how good the sponge bath must feel to her.

When we were done I found a soft pink johnny shirt that made Nakina's skin look less yellow. Nakina didn't speak while we washed her, and when we were done the nurse gave her morphine and she fell asleep. I sat beside the bed, window still open, white curtains blowing in the breeze. I could smell the lavender and soap. I looked across at her face, her elegant nose, her strong cheekbones, and I thought how beautiful she looked.

———◆———

Toivo drove out to the house with me that afternoon. I wanted to talk to him about the barn. When we got to the house he took his tools out of the truck and went into the kitchen. "I'll prime the pump for you," he said. "Let the water run for about a half an hour. The pipes are a mess but that will flush things out."

I watched him work and was excited about having running water. I could hook up a hose and run it out to the field to water the garden. We went out and looked at the barn and Toivo agreed with me. "The supporting beams are solid. They'll be standing for another hundred years," he said.

"Can we knock in some bigger windows back here?"

"No problem. Three, maybe five, right across the back. I had a look at the sauna. You could use a new stove."

"You think so?"

"That one's starting to rust."

"Well, it's pretty old. You want some tea?"

"No, I got beer in the truck."

We took our beers and walked across the field to check out the sauna. It was good to be there with Toivo. I could learn a lot from him.

chapter twenty-six

My exhibition closed at the end of the June. I sold five paintings and the library was interested in buying the Stone Man. I spent a day with Merika taking down the show and packing up the canvases. Most of them were being shipped back to Halifax, but I had decided to keep two of them at the house. And there was one more I didn't pack.

I took the painting of Nakina at the Lorna Doone to the hospital with me and placed it on the floor against the wall where I thought she could see it from her bed. When Nakina woke up she looked at me, then at the painting, and said in a thin voice, "Miigwetch."

I sat quietly with her for a few hours. Every so often she would say something but I wasn't sure if she was speaking to me or to someone in the room who I couldn't see. The veil kept dropping between us.

Just after she fell asleep her body started to shake. I ran for the nurse.

Epileptic seizure. I had forgotten. They wrapped her body in warm blankets, and eventually the seizure passed. "You want another blanket?" I asked.

"Talk to me."

"About what?"

"About Loon Lake. Talk to me about Loon Lake."

I rubbed her shoulder and arm.

"We swam a lot. Remember? And we rowed in the Little Tink. Do you remember the rowboat my dad made?"

"He liked boats."

"And sometimes at night Dad made a bonfire."

"We picked blueberries along the tracks." Nakina said.

"And Mom made pies."

"No, bannock. Blueberry bannock. Lillian taught me how to make blueberry bannock."

"That was in Rocky Lake."

"You were such an asshole sometimes, eh," she said, smiling at me.

I smiled back and kept rubbing her shoulder. She seemed chilled even with all the blankets.

"Molly?"

"Yeah."

"Don't bring any goddamn priests in here OK."

"OK. No priests. I promise."

"I'm not Catholic."

"I know."

"They tried to make me one. At the residential school. Tried to make me into a good little Catholic girl. Made me pray to the new goddamned pope."

"What new pope?" I thought she was slipping behind the veil again.

"First thing I remember when I got to the residential school. There was a new pope and we had to go to the chapel and pray for Pope John."

She slept until the dinner trays arrived. "Do you want me to help you sit up?" I asked.

"No. I'm not hungry."

"You didn't eat any lunch."

"I just want to sleep."

Before I left the hospital that night I stopped at the nursing station and let them know Nakina hadn't touched her dinner. The nurse said it was a sign that her body was getting ready to let go.

Before heading back out to Kamanistiquia I stopped at the library. If Nakina was right, if the first thing she remembered after going to the residential school was the election of Pope John, then at least that would give me a date. Something I could use to go through the school records.

It was strange walking into the library again after so many years. I stood for a few minutes beside the stained glass windows of Charles Dickens and William Shakespeare and I remembered the weird, quiet girl who spent so many hours there. The building looked old. The carpets were worn and the furniture was tired and tattered. I found the World Book Encyclopedia 'P' and looked under popes. I found him:

Angelo Roncalli was ordained a priest in 1904 and served in various posts including appointment as Papal Nuncio in several countries, including France (1944). He did much to help Jews during the Holocaust. Pope Pius XII made Roncalli a Cardinal in 1953. Pope John was elected on 28 October 1958 at the age of 77.

Nineteen fifty-eight. Nakina was almost a year older than me so she would have been about six when she arrived at the residential school. I remembered the records from the residential school—the journals of admissions and discharges. I would search the files to see if I could find a journal of admissions for nineteen fifty-eight.

Lars had four days off and came out to the house with me. Toivo and a friend were working on the barn. They put in the windows along the back wall and were reinforcing the floor. Lars worked with them.

I was out in the garden weeding. It amazed me how hard it was to get things to grow in that damn clay soil, but the weeds seemed to thrive. I could see four lines of green where the potatoes were poking through. We'd have a ton of potatoes in the fall.

That afternoon we installed the new sauna stove. It took four of us to lift it from the back of the truck. It would last a long time.

When Toivo and his friend went back to town at the end of the day, Lars stayed on. At night we stoked up the sauna and christened the new stove. Lars got the fire going and I carried wood. "I can't believe how fast it's heating up," I said. "The old stove would have taken twice as long."

When the sauna was ready we stepped into the outer room and stripped. I wasn't shy like I was the first time I'd been with Lars. We sat up on the top bench and after Lars threw a ladle of water on the stones we sat with our heads down, slowly breathing in the hot steam. I had a bar of birch soap Kikko had given me and I scrubbed my arms. Lars took a cloth, lifted my hair and scrubbed my shoulders and back. I could feel my body relaxing but just as I began to let go, a shiver of guilt ran through me. Not now. I couldn't relax now.

"Talk to me," Lars said. "What's wrong?"

"I don't think I can do it," I said.

"Do what?"

"Help Nakina. I don't know what to do. There's so much pain and I don't know what the fuck to do." I put my head down and tried to think of how to say what I was feeling. "When I'm there, when I'm at the hospital I don't want to be there. That's the truth. I sit for hours and goddamn hours just waiting. I feel like such an idiot sometimes because I don't know how to help. And I can't wait to get away, I can't wait to leave the hospital, and as soon as I leave her I want to go back and be with her. I want to go back and be close to her so she's not alone. I should be there with her now. I need to get this right. I've let her down so many times before, I need to get this right."

Lars put his arms around me and when he threw another ladle of water on the stones I let the steam wash away my tears.

"Maybe all you need is to be there."

"What do you mean?"

"Just be there. Be with her. Maybe that's enough."

When the fire died down Lars wrapped a towel around me, picked me up and carried me to the house. I didn't know until that moment how much I needed to be carried.

That night I dreamt about waking the Stone Man. I dreamt I went down to the wharf with Nakina and I shouted to him. There was a great crashing of rock and he sat up and walked across the water towards us, his footsteps churning up the lake into frothy whitecaps. When he got to the wharf the Stone Man reached his broad hand down and lay it on my head like a blessing. Then he wrapped his granite arms around Nakina's frail body and took her back out into the lake with him. The lake stilled as he lay down to sleep and I was alone on the wharf. The Stone Man had taken his daughter home.

Nakina slept more every day, and when she was awake she seemed far away. She said a lot of things that didn't make sense and sometimes spoke to people who weren't there. Sometimes she'd speak in English, then say a few words in Ojibwe. I'd hold her hand and she'd say something to me, then something to people I couldn't see, then she'd talk to me like I could hear what they just said.

I sat and held her hand and let her take me into that strange in between place where she was travelling. It felt peaceful. And in that place of in-between I sometimes felt the presence of my mother and father. There was an energy around us. I didn't try to understand it—it was enough just to be there.

I was getting used to the rhythm of the hospital, the long periods of quiet, then the flurry of activity before a change of shift. I got to know the best time to ask for things and when not to bother the nurses. I knew the names of all the cleaning staff and they made such a fuss over Nakina. I was touched by the small kindnesses I saw every day. And I found out what those funny little toothette things were that I'd seen in the bathroom. The nurse taught me how to wet them with water and rinse out the inside of Nakina's mouth and moisten her lips. It felt good to do something useful.

Mitch and his wife Marcia and some people from the Friendship Centre came to visit. One day they brought Mr. Bannon, an elder from the Fort McKay reserve. They brought sweetgrass for a smudging ceremony. Marcia and I stood near the door in case a nurse tried to come in. We didn't think they would approve. Mr. Bannon lit the dried sweetgrass in a shallow stone bowl and with a feather he fanned the smoke over Nakina. He and Mitch spoke some prayers in Ojibwe and Nakina looked to be at peace. For hours afterwards I could smell the musky scent of the sweetgrass.

There were flowers from Anna, Kiiko and Toivo, and some cards from people she'd worked with in British Colombia. She asked me to read the cards and letters to her, and I could see Nakina had made an impact in their lives when she was out west. She had made a good life there.

Sometimes when Nakina slept I'd stretch out in the chair and look out the window at the Stone Man. I thought about all the years we had lost.

"Water. I need water." Nakina was awake and seemed agitated.

I got a fresh jug of ice water and moistened Nakina's lips.

"I saw the northern lights," she said, "when I lived in the mountains. They were beautiful."

"I could see them out at my place in Kamanistiquia," I said.

"Your house. I like it."

"I've moved back out there. I'm living there now."

"Alone?"

"I have a friend. He stays with me sometimes."

"Is he nice?"

"Very nice. He's very…" I thought about how to describe Lars. "Kind. He's very kind and gentle."

I hoped she would say more, but she drifted off to sleep.

She was asleep when I arrived the next morning and there was an oxygen mask over her face. The room was still. A nurse came to the door and asked to see me at the nursing station.

"She slipped into a coma last night," the nurse said. "She's not in any pain. She may stay like this for a few days. She might regain consciousness. It's hard to say."

"What can I do?"

"Sit with her. Talk to her. She may still be able to hear you, know you're there."

I went back into the room and sat on the chair beside Nakina. Her body was there and I could see her chest rising and falling. But she was far away. I tried to talk to her but I didn't know what to say. Maybe it had all been said.

I stayed silently beside her, holding her hand, watching her chest rise and fall until her breathing stilled and she was gone.

———◈———

The day after the cremation I drove out to Kamanistiquia with Nakina's ashes in an urn on the seat beside me. There was no funeral. She didn't want that. No ceremony, no one there except me and Mitch standing together on the cement floor at the back of the crematorium. As the door to the furnace opened and the pine box holding her body moved forward Mitch's arm rose suddenly in an arched swooping gesture like a bird taking flight and as her body was fed into the flames I felt Nakina's soul rise and take flight. Free.

At the house I placed the silver urn on the kitchen table and poured myself a glass of wine. I looked up at the painting Celeste had done. *Summer*—the pure joy of a child. I looked at the painting of Nakina out in the boat with Dad—Dad's curly hair blowing back in the wind and his hand on the throttle of the engine. Nakina with the wind whipping her hair across her face and that silly grin on her face. That grin. I looked at the tiny black shoe from the rubble of the residential school. A reminder of all the children who had been lost.

I got out the box with the photocopies from the residential school, lit the Coleman lamp and began to sort through the copies of the ledgers. There were no copies for 1958. The last I had were from 1943. I turned the dial on the lamp to raise the wick so I could see. The writing was very faint. So many names—Lillian Sabourine, Hubert Moses, Gilbert Sabourine, Rose Jackpine—entries in a journal that might be the only proof these children existed, the only link left between these children and the families they had been taken from. They came from all across Northern Ontario—Perrault Falls, Red Lake, Armstrong, Sandy Lake. I wondered where they were now. I wondered how many had found their way home. How many families were broken forever?

When Nakina was taken from her family the thread of her life story was broken. Who was her mother? Her father? Did she have brothers or sisters? If she had a sister was she tough and smart like Nakina? Did they work the trap lines? What did her grandmother look like? Were they funny? Were they serious? Were they religious—what did they believe?

I remembered how Nakina would sit at the kitchen table asking Mom a million questions about our family. She was searching my family for stories because the thread to hers was broken.

I had a small piece of Nakina's story. All I could do for now was hold it safe. I'd hold it safe until I could find more. I had a date. There were more records in the library archives. There might be a way to trace back to her family.

There were things I knew—that she was my friend and my sister and she was smart and funny and could be a real pain in the ass too. The fun we had at Loon Lake and how we used to read Leonard Cohen and write his poems on the board at school and how she wore pink lipstick and loved the Beatles. I'd remember that her Anishinaabe name was Waawaashkeshi. I'd remember the hard stuff too, about the residential school and abuse. The rape. What they did to her. That was her story too. I'd keep it safe.

I put the papers back in the box and walked across the kitchen. The screen door creaked when it opened. I walked behind the house out into the moonlit field.

I had my painting of Nakina at the Lorna Doone and the photos she took at Rocky Lake and the photo of us together in the rowboat at Loon Lake. I had a piece of her life and I would hold it safe. And I would keep looking for answers. Maybe someday I could get on a train heading north and take her home.

Nakina was right. You can always get home. The tracks run both ways.

author note

grew up in Thunder Bay, in the shadow of the Sleeping Giant. In writing this novel I took elements of Thunder Bay combined with several other towns in Northern Ontario to create the fictional community of Fort McKay. Although I left Northern Ontario in my late teens, the fierce beauty of Lake Superior's north shore continues to haunt me.

Like Molly, I was a young girl who stood silently outside the fence of the residential school looking in. Over time I asked questions and came to learn that what I was witnessing represented one of the darkest chapters of Canadian history.

For over a century over 150,000 Aboriginal children were removed from their families and sent to residential schools. The result of the physical and emotional abuse suffered by so many continues to impact future generations. In 2008 Prime Minister Harper apologized on behalf of the Canadian government and asked the "forgiveness of the Aboriginal peoples of this country for failing them so profoundly." Through the work of the Truth and Reconciliation Commission of Canada the survivors of the residential school system have been given voice and a national journey of healing has begun.

acknowledgements

I would like to extend my deep gratitude to the visionaries who created the Beacon Award for Social Justice Literature. Thank you for your belief in the power of fiction to inspire and change the world. To the distinguished jury members who gave of their time and provided invaluable feedback, my humble thanks.

To Bev Rach for her confidence in the book, Chris Benjamin for giving me a stronger voice, Brenda Conroy for polishing my words and the whole fabulous Roseway team, my heartfelt thanks.

This is a novel about friendship and love. For bringing that into my life I am deeply grateful to my beloved family, and my beloved family of friends.

book club notes

1. As the novel opens Molly sees Nakina attempting to escape from the residential school. Why do you think Nakina was trying to escape when she did not know where home was, and punishment was certain if she were caught?

2. When Molly is out on the lake in her father's boat she looks back at the city and sees the invisible lines of class and race that separate the town. Do you think similar invisible lines of social distinction exist in your community?

3. The Sleeping Giant, or Stone Man plays a central role in the novel both as geographical landscape and mythological being. In legend the Sleeping Giant watched over and protected the Ojibwe people until he was turned to stone. What do you think is the significance of the title *Wake the Stone Man*?

4. Molly is witness to Nakina's attack but stays silent. Why do you think she didn't or couldn't tell the truth of what she saw?

5. Finding family is a major theme in the novel, central to both Molly and Nakina's journey. Do you think, in the end, they found family?

6. A strong friendship is forged between Molly and Nakina when they are in their teens. How do you think this bond endured through tragedy and years of separation?

7. *Wake the Stone Man* is set in the 1970s at a time when much of the truth of the horrific abuse in residential schools was hidden or denied. Since 2008 the Truth and Reconciliation Commission of Canada has held hearings across Canada, giving voice to the survivors of the residential school system. Do you think the work of the TRC in bringing the truth to light will help the journey towards healing?

The Beacon Award
for Social Justice Literature

The Beacon Award for Social Justice Literature is a prize for
an unpublished novel. Its purpose is to stimulate the creation,
publication and dissemination of new works of fiction designed
to ignite readers' passion for and understanding of social justice.
The Beacon Award is appreciative of all its individual
supporters and also thanks Hignell Book Printing
and Michael Nuschke and Richard Nickerson of
Assante Capital Management for their generous support.

Visit beaconaward.ca for more information